SOUTHWELL MINSTER.

AN ACCOUNT OF THE

Collegiate and Cathedral Church

OF

SOUTHWELL,

ARCHITECTURAL,

ARCHÆOLOGICAL,

AND

HISTORICAL,

BY

GREVILE MAIRIS LIVETT, B.A.,

S. JOHN'S COLL. CAMB.

Assistant-Master at Spondon House School, near Derby.

SOUTHWELL:
JOHN WHITTINGHAM, QUEEN STREET.
1883.

PREFACE.

No apology need be offered for the appearance of this little work at a time when Southwell is in the minds of all who have the welfare of our Church at heart. It has occupied the leisure of the writer for some months, and he only regrets that time and distance have combined to prevent his working out the subject as thoroughly as he wished. Probably it would not have been undertaken but for the labours in the same field of Mr. Dimock, the editor of the *Magna Vita S. Hugonis* in the series of the Master of the Rolls, and for some years a Vicar Choral of the Collegiate Church of Southwell. Mr. Dimock, however, confined his attention to the fabric and its history, so that for materials for the history of the College of Secular Canons the writer has had to look elsewhere. MSS. in the British Museum and the Public Record Office have been consulted with advantage, together with the State Papers and such books of reference as came to hand. But the Chartas granted to the Canons by the Archbishops of York, and the Statutes of Queen Elizabeth, have been the chief sources of information. They are preserved in a MS. belonging to the Church, entitled *The Statutes*, and printed both in Dugdale's *Monasticon* and in the Appendix to Dickenson's *History of the Antiquities of Southwell*. The latter work, which first appeared in 1787, is to be read with caution, its chief value lying in the Appendix. The author was the son of a Vicar-general of the College, and himself a chorister. Other local histories, one by Shilton, published in 1818, and a third by Clarke and Killpack in 1838, are little more than abridgments of Mr. Dickenson's work. The Church was despoiled of all its muniments and early records during the troubles of the 16th and 17th centuries, and the only MS. of any importance that has come down to us besides *The Statutes* is the *Registrum Album* or White Book of Southwell. The writer has had no opportunity of consulting this MS., but it seems to have yielded all its treasures to the industry of Mr. Dickenson and Mr. Dimock successively. A general history of our ancient Secular Colleges, which would form an interesting work, seems never to have been taken in hand, but many valuable hints have been gained from Mr. E. A. Freeman's Lectures on the *Cathedral Church of Wells*.

Special thanks are due to the Rev. R. F. Smith, not only for the use of his notes from the later *Chapter Records*, but also for his kind explanation of many difficult points, more especially historical. Also to Mr. Hamilton Browne, for his valuable help in correcting the proof-sheets of the architectural description of the fabric. The kindness must be acknowledged of Mr. Bloxam and Mr. James Parker for communicating information with regard to subjects on which experience has made them authorities. Throughout the work full reference is made in the foot-notes to the works of other writers in cases where their words or opinions are quoted in the text. The index is by no means a general one, being meant merely to facilitate reference to the descriptive parts of the book, and to direct attention to the more important points in the history of Southwell and its Canons. The drawings are most of them taken from photographs; these, with the plans, have been reproduced by Mr. Cowell's anastatic printing process. It only remains to add that, owing to the necessity of hastening forward the publication of the work, a number of errors have been allowed to remain in the text, only the most important of which have been corrected by the insertion of a list of *errata*.

Spondon, Derby,
November, 1883.

TABLE OF CONTENTS.

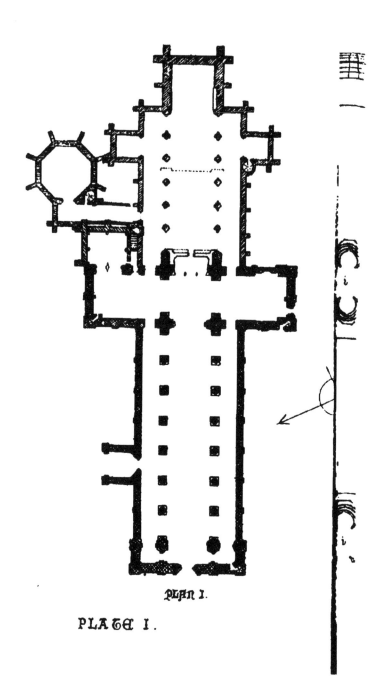

PLAN I.

PLATE I.

LIST AND CONTENTS OF PLATES.

PLATE I.

N.B.—The dates are given in round numbers. The following will explain the use of the dots : the Choir was in building between the years 1230 and 1250 ; it may have been begun before 1230, but 1250 is the latest date that can be assigned for its completion.

PLAN II.—Ground-plan of Norman Church (restored).

PLAN III.—Ground-plan and Elevation of remains of Apse at East end of North Choir-aisle in Norman Church.

NORMAN WORK.	LATER WORK.
a. Ashlar walling.	*g.* Doorway to Chapter-house.
b. Quoin.	*h.* Early Eng. doorway and steps.
c. Rough-stone foundation.	*i.* Early English piers.
d. Rubble.	
e. Plinth.	
f. Old paving.	

PLATE II.

PLATE III.

PLATE IV.

ERRATA.

Page 1*, *for* E. H. Freeman *read* E. A. Freeman.
,, 2, line 1, *for* 1545 *read* 1547.
,, 21, line 8, *for* north *read* south.
,, 23*, *for* Roma *read* Romanus.
,, 28. *On chantries see note on p.* 127.
,, 32, line 15, *for* 1541 *read* 1547.
,, 32‡, *for* Professor Willis *read* Brown Willis.
,, 36, line 8, *for* 1579 *read* 1585.
,, 39, line 11, *strike out* the date of the Elizabethan Statutes.
,, 49, line 8, *for* £3,500 *read* £3,000.
,, 56, line 28, *for* is *read* are.
,, 101*, *for fleur read fleurs.*
,, 124†, *for* Haines *read* Cutts.
,, 133, *for* Idolatris *read* Idolatras.
,, 140, line 2, *for* duobos *read* duobus.

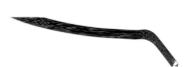

CHAPTER I.

HISTORY AND CONSTITUTION OF THE COLLEGIATE
CHURCH.

At the outset some explanation of the title—The Collegiate and Cathedral Church of Southwell—seems necessary. The history of this church in the past is that of a collegiate church: its future history will be that of a cathedral. An Act of Parliament passed early in the present reign deprived it of its collegiate character, while another and later act has made it the mother church of a new diocese, consisting of the counties of Nottingham and Derby, which have hitherto belonged to the dioceses of Lincoln and Lichfield respectively. Funds are now being raised to found the bishopric, and until this is accomplished the church is merely parochial. A church is called a cathedral, or more properly speaking a cathedral church, when it contains the *throne* of a bishop, who takes the title of his *see* from the name of the town or city in which it stands. In fact the word *cathedral* is an adjective derived from the Greek and Latin *cathedra*, which means a *seat*, and exists in our language in the form *chair*.* A collegiate church, on the other hand, is one belonging to a *college*, or *collected* body, of priests called secular canons, as opposed to regular canons, and not necessarily containing the throne of a bishop. Before the suppression of these colleges in the reign of Edward VI., a great number of them existed throughout the country.† Beverley Minster was a collegiate church, and St. Stephen's, Westminster, the present Houses of Parliament, another. The Chapel of S. Mary and S. George at Windsor is still collegiate, for it was particularly excepted

---

* Dr. E. H. Freeman's *Wells*, where this and similar points are explained.   † See Dugdale's *Monasticon Anglicanum*.

from the act of 1545. A few of them were refounded soon
after the suppression, as in the cases of Southwell and Manchester. Manchester and Ripon, both formerly collegiate,
have in our own times been raised to the dignity of episcopal
sees; while there are many instances of churches, like Lichfield and York, which from the earliest ages have been both
collegiate and cathedral combined, the double character saving
them untouched by the act of suppression.

The distinction, too, between *secular* clergy and *regular*
clergy must be clearly understood. Jerome tells us that as
early as the 3rd century after Christ there were in Egypt
Coenobites, or monks who lived in common. During the
middle ages many orders of monks sprung into existence and
established themselves in our islands, the most famous of which
were the Benedictine and Cistercian Orders. The monks were
at first all laymen, and spent their whole lives within the
walls of their monasteries;* but in time many of them took
holy orders, and going abroad among the people busied themselves in missionary work. They still, however, continued
to live strictly according to the *regulus* or rule of the order
to which they were attached, wherefore they have been styled
regular clergy, to distinguish them from the *secular* priests,
or parochial clergy, who, acknowledging no rule except the
law of the land, lived amongst the people, and were often
married men. From very early times, however, there seem to .
have been communities of secular clergy also, who banded
themselves together for religious devotion or other purpose.
Athanasius† evidently referred to such when, writing in the
4th century, he said he "knew of monks who both ate and
drank, and were the fathers of families;" but we should
not call such men monks nowadays. Such communities
grew at length into colleges of secular priests, like the one at
Southwell. The priests of a college like Southwell resembled
monks inasmuch as they had a rule of life, they worshipped
in one church, and owned common property; but they were
unlike monks in that they took no vow like the triple monastic
vow of poverty, chastity, and obedience, nor did they live in

---

* At the suppression of the monasteries in the reign of Henry
VIII. all the domestic buildings were destroyed, while the churches
attached to them were in many cases left standing for parochial use;
but enough still remains of the former to enable their form and
general arrangement to be recovered.   † *Ep. ad Dracont.*

common, but apart with their families in their own private houses.

Here we may explain the different application of the terms canon and prebendary. Every member of the collegiate body was at the same time a canon and a prebendary. As a member of the chapter he was called a canon, and he was also a prebendary in that he owned a *præbenda* or prebend, that is to say a separate estate. The canons of the college as a corporate body formed the *chapter*, and when they met together to discuss matters relating to their church or the affairs of their common property, the meeting was called a chapter-meeting, and the place where they met the chapter-house. In many instances the canons of secular colleges possessed only common property at first, and after a time the custom prevailed of dividing a part of it among the canons individually, or else it was that benefactors arose who founded prebends with fresh grants of land without drawing from the common stock.

It is difficult to fix a date for the foundation of the church at Southwell. That it held an important position in the diocese of York before the Norman Conquest is certain, and the question remains did it exist before the Danish invasion in the 9th century. I think we shall, on examination, find it probable that there was a church here long before the 9th century, though nothing beyond its mere existence is known of it In all likelihood it was destroyed by the Danes, itself having been the successor of one built on the same spot during the Roman occupation of Britain. Tradition points to S. Paulinus as the founder of a church here—the founder alike of York and Lincoln, the friend and companion of S. Augustine, the great missionary of Northumbria under King Edwin, and the first Archbishop of York, A.D. 627-633. This tradition rests upon statements to this effect contained in certain *private histories* of the church which are no longer extant. They are quoted, however, by Camden in his *Magna Britannia*, which first appeared in 1586, and were possibly lost during the civil wars of the following century, when most of the church records were either destroyed or for safety carried away.*
They tell us how S. Paulinus founded the church at Southwell when he was baptizing the people of this district in the Trent. And a careful consideration of the Venerable Bede's account of

---

* As appears from the Rolls' Court Book.

4

the missionary work of S. Paulinus gives support to the statement. The ecclesiastical historian makes no direct reference to Southwell, but internal evidence in his account of Paulinus' missionary work, more especially the evidence of the place-names mentioned, is strong in favour of the view that Paulinus extended his labours to the close neighbourhood of Southwell. This being the case, there will be little reason to doubt the authenticity of the statements of Camden's private histories. What does Bede say? The gist of his narrative is as follows:—"Paulinus also preached the word to the "province of Lindsey, which is the first province on the south "bank of the Humber, extending to the sea, and converted "the governor of Lincoln, Blæcca by name, and his house- "hold. In which city he built a stately stone church, and "consecrated Honorius bishop. With regard to the faith of "this province, a certain Priest and Abbot of the monastery "of Partaneu,* named Deda, a man of singular veracity, told "me that one of the oldest persons living informed him that "he himself and a great crowd of people had been baptized "at mid-day by Bishop Paulinus, in the presence of King "Edwin, in the river Trent, near a city called in the English "tongue Tiovulfingacester." Authorities are divided as to the identity of this Tiovulfingacester, so that, for the present at least, we must assume that it is not in the immediate neighbourhood of Southwell. We notice here that Bede evidently does not pretend to give a 'detailed or exhaustive account of Paulinus' missionary travels; in fact he does not seem to have had much information to write upon. But from this and other passages in the same author we gather that his travels were very extensive, stretching over a period of some years probably; and, because Bede says that he preached to the people of Lindsey, there is no reason to believe that his labours were confined to that province, the precise limits of which the historian was probably not acquainted with. Paulinus worked up the valley of the Trent southwards, and diverging to Lincoln, founded the church there, and converted Blæcca the governor. A further journey of about thirty miles along the Trent from its nearest point to Lincoln, and of only twenty miles direct from that city by the Foss Way, would bring him to Bleasby and Fiskerton, situate on the river only three or four miles from Southwell. The name

* A cell of Bardney Abbey : Deda was the first abbot.

Bleasby is the key to the whole position. Bede tells us that
King Edwin accompanied Paulinus in this missionary journey,
and no doubt his new convert Blæcca was also of his company.
And the name Bleasby at once suggests a contraction of
Blæccasby.* Possibly this was the very spot where the
governor of Lincoln received the rites of baptism, an event
perpetuated in the name of the settlement there. And when,
on looking again at the map, we find a place called Edwinstow
only a few miles north of Southwell, the position is immensely
strengthened. *Stow* is a common form of the A. S. *stoc*, a
stockaded place, and the fitness of the name Edwinstow, or
King Edwin's stockade (with which we may compare Chep-
stow, the stockaded market-place; and Bristol, anciently
Bricgstow, the stockaded bridge), is immediately seen when
we remember that this was on the limits of the King's
domain, where he would feel the necessity of protection
against any hostile movement on the part of an unfriendly
population. It is quite possible, therefore, that Paulinus,
accompanied by Edwin and Blæcca, reached that part of the
Trent that flows within four miles of Southwell; and if so,
it requires no stretch of imagination to believe that he then
founded a church at Southwell. The theory here advanced
may by itself seem problematic, and we have no wish to hide
its weak points; but when considered in connection with the
positive statements of the private histories of Southwell to
which Camden had access it becomes even a probable one.

* *By* is the very common Norse suffix meaning originally " an
"abode or single farm, and hence it afterwards came to denote a
"village."—Taylor.

Note.—There is one other argument which I have already hinted
at, and it is one which the friend who has kindly unfolded it
to me, and who has paid a good deal of attention to the question,
considers to have some weight. It is the much-contested identity
of Bede's Tiovulfingacester. Dr. Stukely places it at Torksey,
the point where the Foss Dyke, which connects the Witham and
the Trent, and forms the S.W. boundary of the province of
Lindsey, joins the latter river. In placing it here the topogra-
pher is influenced, I believe, by two facts—first that it is the
nearest point on the Trent to Lincoln, and secondly that it is within
the province of Lindsey. I do not believe that Bede's topographical
knowledge was sufficiently accurate to necessitate our placing it
within Lindsey. Camden, who is blindly followed by Dugdale and
many other writers, identifies it with Southwell. On this, Mr.
Dimock writes: " The Southwell history said that St. Paulinus
" baptized the people of Nottingham in the Trent, and founded the

I must not omit to notice a curious MS. among the records which Mr. Dimock brought to light, entitled "Simposium, "contayning a dialogue touching the state of the church of "Southwell." "It was written," he says, "in the year 1604 "or '5 by a prebendary of the church evidently well versed "in its history: most of its statements can be verified from "other sources of undoubted authority." In this MS. the following passage occurs:—" If I fetch the antiquity of the "church no further than that learned godly antiquary Mr. "Cambden hath done, although it come far short, yet it may "easily thereby appear, as otherwise, that there was, many "hundred years past, a collegiate and parochial church at South- "well." Besides this passage we have no written evidence of the ancient British church which is implied in the words "although it come far short." It is certain, however, that in the foundations of the present structure many fragments of

"church of Southwell: Bede had said that he baptized the people of "Lindsey in the Trent, near Tiovulfingacester. It would surely be "no safe logic hence to conclude that Tiovulfingacester and South- "well are one." Let us consider the etymon of the name. The latter part is of course the Roman *castra* or camp. This leaves *Tiovulfinga*, in which the syllable *ing* is the common Saxon patronymic. There are more than two thousand place-names in England bearing this patronymic: there are thirty-five in Notting-hamshire; in fact Nottingham itself is the *home* of the Anglo-Saxon tribe of the *Snotingas*. *Tiovulf* then was the founder of the family of Tiovulfingas; and the place where they settled, having been once a Roman camp and bearing the name castra, they called Tiovulfinga-cester. But Henry of Huntingdon writes it undoubtedly Fingacestre: by his time (12th century) the *Tiovul* had been dropped. This would doubtless be pronounced Fincster or Ficster, a contraction which Mr. Taylor, in his *Words and Places*, has proved to have taken place in all names compounded of *castra* which occur in Mercian parts of the kingdom, as in Leicester, Worcester, Cirencester, which is pronounced Sister or Siseter. Then, as in the cases of Casterton, Chesterton, when the place became more considerable the affix *ton* would be given it, which would make it pronounced Ficsterton, which, by a natural interchange of consonants, became Fiskerton. The chief objection to this derivation, which is quite possible from an etymological point of view, is the fact that the Domesday Book has Fiscartune; and this, of course, is of earlier date than Henry of Huntingdon If, on the other hand, it can be accepted, the theory that Paulinus founded a church at Southwell, resting on the direct testimony of the private histories, and supported by the combined evidence of the names, Fiskerton, Bleasby, and Edwinstow, is still further strength-ened.

Roman brick have been found, which gives it material support; and though of course it would be swept away in the Anglo-Saxon invasion and occupation of this part of the country, its existence supplies a reason for the choice of the spot by S. Paulinus whereon to found his church. Of the constitution of the church of S. Paulinus we know nothing, unless we may accept the authority of the Simposium again, which styles it "collegiate and parochial." I do not mean, of course, that S. Paulinus there and then fixed the number of priests, formed them into a college, and gave them common property. This would be assuming an advanced state of church organisation wholly incompatible with the character of his mission. A study of the Notts. place-names shews that the Anglian settlements followed the Trent within a very few miles of the river; and the forest-land of the interior must have been left in the possession of the wild beasts. The church would be established merely as a missionary centre for the conversion of the heathen settlers along the Trent valley; and the spot chosen just at the bend of the river was a convenient one for the purpose. One or two priests, perhaps, were left there to carry on the work of the mission. The number would grow as the sphere of labour widened, and at some future time they might obtain property and form themselves into a college. Possibly this is what actually did take place, but no such colleges seem to have existed much earlier than the middle of the 8th century.

I have already mentioned the likelihood that any church of Paulinus' foundation fell before the ruthless invasion of the Danes in the 9th century. The fierce Northmen entertained feelings of intense hatred towards the religion which had supplanted the worship of their deities, Thor and Woden, in the land which their Anglo-Saxon kinsmen and enemies had made their own; and their destroying arm swept away all traces of Christianity from those parts of the country which they scoured. The number of place-names which bear the suffixes *thorpe* and *by*, which denote permanent Danish settlements occurring in the neighbourhood of Newark and Southwell, clearly shew how thoroughly the Danes colonized the district; and that the village of Southwell itself offered special attractions to them we have a lasting witness in the two hamlets of East Thorpe and West Thorpe; while its streets once bore the historic names of Prest-gate and Potter-

gate, Milne-gate and Ferthingate,* which last has given place
to the meaningless name of King-street. Mr. Freeman dates
the conquest of this part of Mercia about 877. Assuming
then that the church of S. Paulinus was destroyed at this
time, when and by whom was it refounded? It is a note-
worthy fact that as soon as the fury of their first onslaughts
had spent itself the Danes allowed themselves to be converted
to the religion of the people among whom they settled. In
illustration of this we may remind our readers that Guthrum,
the first Danish King of East Anglia, embraced Christianity
within three weeks from the peace of Wedmore. The church
then may have been re-established almost immediately, but
the very unsettled state of Mercia from this time certainly
up to Edgar's reign, as well as the little more particular
evidence we have, favours a later date. The close connection
of Wulstan, archbishop of York, with the Danish revolt of
948, leads one to suppose that by this time the Danes were
completely Christianised.† This brings us close to the date I
venture to propose to for the new foundation—viz. 957 or '8.
The evidence is certainly not overwhelming, but it is such as
seems to me well worth considering. The two points are
these: first, in the certificate of the commissioners, 37 Henry
VIII., extant in the Public Record Office, the foundation is
ascribed, on the evidence of three of the prebendaries of the
church, to "the Righte famous of memorye Edgare the
Kinge ma^ties moste noble p'genitor." Secondly, in the Cod.
Dip. Ævi Sax. is preserved an instrument of King Edwy,
dated 958, granting to Oscytel, archbishop of York, the crown
lands at Suthwell. On the first blush one is inclined to discredit the evidence of the three prebendaries,‡ the argument
at once presenting itself that it is very unlikely that Edgar,
who owed his crown to the action of the Benedictine monks,
would in this single exception follow the policy which in
reality cost his brother Edwy both crown and life. But the

---

* The Danish *gata* means a street or road. The names of all the
older streets in Peterborough, Lincoln, York, Leeds, and in fact in
all the towns in Norse parts of England, bear this suffix. The A.S.
geat means a gate.

† Both Oskytel, Wulstan's successor, and Odo, the Abp. of Canterbury, were of Danish families.

‡ One of these, a Mr. Adams, we shall hear more about: he was
not altogether a bright character.

objection falls to the ground on a closer examination of dates and names. The historical position is this—

955. Edwy becomes king, and Edgar reigns as under-king in Mercia.

956. Dunstan banished by Edwy, whereupon in

957. The Mercians and Northumbrians, at the instigation of Odo, Abp. of Canterbury, revolt from Edwy's over-lordship: they proclaim Edgar their independent king, and Dunstan is summoned home by Edgar to his court.

958. Date of "Instrument of Edwy" making grant to Oskytel. Odo divorces Edwy and Elgiva. Odo's death.

959. Edwy dies: Edgar, now 16 years old, becomes King of all England, and Dunstan succeeds Odo as Abp. of Canterbury.

Here we notice that Edgar was independent King of Mercia in 957. His extreme youth, as well as what we know of his personal character, makes it unlikely that he had become the avowed champion of the monks at this time—in fact his part in the systematic war against the secular clergy, which was in reality played *for* him by Dunstan, was not begun until he became King of all England in 959—and, as the secular clergy still formed a strong party in his realms,* it is easy to imagine that the young King of Mercia may have acceded to a wish on the part of his new subjects for the foundation of a secular college at the fallen church of Southwell, while Dunstan's position at his court was not yet sufficiently assured to warrant him in offering any resistance to his will. The grant of Edwy, shortly afterwards, to Oscytel, himself it seems a secular, implies the existence of a church at Southwell in 958. It is by no means improbable that Edwy was compelled to make this grant; at any rate the fact that Edgar himself subscribed the grant is very significant, while the name of Odo—Odo the Severe, who was more cruel and fanatical in his opposition to the seculars than even Dunstan himself—appears confirming the same. On the whole there seems to be no ground for rejecting the point-blank assertion of the three prebendaries in the certificate of 37 Henry VIII. that Edgar founded the Collegiate Church at Southwell.

---

* In Canon Raine's opinion the Benedictine rule was never firmly established here till after the conquest.—See Mr. Ormsby's *York*.

We gather from notices in the writings of Thomas Stubbs and Godwin* that there was a church of considerable size and importance at Southwell shortly before the conquest, while Thomas Stubbs directly implies the existence at that time of a collegiate body of canons here, though, as we have seen, we have reason to believe the college to have been a much older institution. He tells us that Aldred, archbishop of York from 1061 to 1069, purchased lands at his own costs, and with them formed prebends at Southwell; and that he also built refectories wherein the canons might take their meals together, one at York and another at Southwell.† This action on the part of Aldred may have been due to the influence of the stricter discipline of the Benedictine order, which was felt more or less by all collegiate bodies about this time, though it affected the north of England far less than the south, and Aldred was the last man to enforce it upon his canons. In some parts of France the canons of secular colleges were subject to all the rules which governed monastic bodies, and differed from monks only by their right of possessing individual property. This was especially the case in Lorraine, where Chrodegang, bishop of Metz, had, in 747, drawn up a very strict code of rules for the government of his college ‡ This is the earliest known instance, I believe, of the establishment of a secular college, properly so called. About the time of the conquest it appears there were as many as ten§ prebends at Southwell, but I have not been able to trace the particulars of their several foundations; though I believe the information is forthcoming shortly through the researches of another writer. In the reign of Henry I. the church of Southwell assumed a prominent position in the diocese of York. The area of the diocese, originally co-extensive with the kingdom of Northumbria, was enormous; and the distance of its outlying portions from the mother church at York, and the difficulties of communication, tended to cut

---

* Thomas Stubbs, in *Twysden's X Scriptores*, biographer of the Archbishops of York.—Godwin, *De Præsulibus*.

† The same prelate founded several prebends at Beverley.—Leland's Collect.—The early history of Beverley is closely allied to that of Southwell.

‡ D'Achery's Spicilegium.

§ By the year 1289 this number had become increased to sixteen, at which it remained fixed. A full list will be given later on.

off the influence of the archbishop and his chapter from the
parishes lying in them. The county of Nottingham manifestly
laboured under this disadvantage, and to remedy it Southwell
was raised to the dignity of the mother church of this part of
the diocese. This took place in the archiepiscopacy of Thomas
II., 1109-1114; and at the same time the entire rebuilding
of the fabric of the church on a larger scale was begun. Of
this archbishop, we read* that he got from King Henry I.,
for the prebends of S Mary of Southwell, the same liberties
as the prebends of S. Peter of York, S. John of Beverley,
and S. Wilfrid of Ripon already possessed; and, so far as to
him pertained, he granted freedom from all episcopal custom
and exaction in their churches and estates. In a letter† to his
parishioners throughout the county of Notts. he speaks of
how he was releasing them from the annual visitations to the
church of York incumbent upon all his other parishioners,
and was allowing them instead to visit the church of S. Mary
of Suwell. This annual visitation was important among the
privileges enjoyed by all mother churches throughout the
kingdom,‡ privileges which seem to have been at this time
granted in full to the Collegiate Church at Southwell, as they
had already been granted to the churches of Ripon and
Beverley. From this time these churches, with that of York,
ranked as the four mother churches of the diocese; and in the
ancient Bidding Prayer, according to the York use,§ the
people were bidden to pray specially for "all the brether and
"sisters of our moder kirke saynt Petvr house of York, saynt
"John house of Beverlay, saynt Wilfride of Rypon, and
"saynt Mary of Suthwell." Again, in the certificate of the
commissioners, 37 Henry VIII., the Collegiate Church of
Suthwell is said to be "reputed and taken as the head mother
"church of the town and countie of Nottingham." Every
year, then, at the Feast of Pentecost, the clergy and laity of
the whole county of Nottingham‖ repaired to the church at
Southwell "with solemn procession, bringing with them the

---

* Thomas Stubbs.   † Registrum Album.

‡ Thorn, in *Twysden's X Scriptores.*   § Drake's Eboracum.

‖ The Mayor and Corporation of Nottingham, with the Justices of
the Peace, in comparatively recent times kept up the custom of
making the journey on horseback, with their best livery on.—Shilton's
History of Southwell.

"Pentecostals,* or Whitsun-farthings as they are sometimes
"called, which were duly paid over to the representative of
"the chapter in the north porch." Referring to a similar
Pentecostal procession at Canterbury, Thorn says, "the
"clergy and people make a publick and solemn procession,
"with their oblations and other devotions, according to the
"custom observed in the mother churches throughout the
"kingdom." Once a year, too, a synod was held at Southwell, answering, doubtless, to the diocesan synod held once
and sometimes twice a year by every bishop in his own
diocese. Almost all the clergy of the diocese, and one spe-
cially-elected layman from each parish, used to attend these
synods. They came in solemn procession to the church ; and,
after a service held there and a charge delivered by the bishop,
inquiry was made into the state and condition of the parishes
and complaints heard by him ; and lastly the general affairs
of the diocese were considered, and the bishop delivered his
own diocesan constitutions for confirmation, which henceforth
became law. Possibly the archbishop presided at the annual
synod at Southwell, and in his absence he would be represented by the chapter in the person of one of the canons
resident. It was at the annual synod, probably, that the
chrism or holy oil (anciently used in baptism, confirmation,
orders, and extreme unction), which had been brought from
the church of York, after having been duly consecrated, was
delivered into the hands of the rural deans, to be distributed
by them to the various parishes in the county. The county
was split up into deaneries. To the following list I have
appended the amount paid by each to the chapter of Southwell
as Pentecostal oblations, as given in Thoroton's and Dickenson's histories—

---

* The Pentecostal offerings were a small sum of money paid by
each parish in the county to Southwell as the mother church. In
olden times they were paid in the north porch of the church, and
afterwards collected by the apparitor at the several visitations. The
payments were continued to the time of the suppression 40 years ago,
and the chapter-clerk attended in the porch every Whitsun-Monday
as a matter of form.—See Shilton.

A tenth-part of the Pentecostals went to the sacristan prebend,
and the residue was equally divided between the commons of the
resident canons and the prebend of Normanton.—Thoroton's *Nottinghamshire.*

The Deanery of	Nottingham	......	£3	9	0
,,	,,	,, Bingham	....	3	2	4
,,	,,	,, Newark	....	3	16	7
,,	,,	,, Retford	....	3	10	2
The Jurisdiction of	Southwell	....	2	0	6

Total £15 18 7

In these and like matters the influence of the church and canons was felt throughout the whole county of Nottingham. But the exercise of episcopal functions which the archbishops granted to the canons as a capitular body was confined to a smaller area. This was called the Peculiar Jurisdiction of Southwell. Such parishes or districts as were exempt from the jurisdiction of the ordinary of the diocese in which they stood used to be called *Peculiars*; it was not that they were subject to no ordinary, but that they had a peculiar ordinary, one of their own that is. In our case the chapter was the ordinary, acting as the archbishop's vicar-general so to speak, while the extent of the peculiar comprised just as much of the county as was in the actual possession of the chapter, or in which the prebendal estates of the canons lay. The only episcopal functions which the chapter could not perform were the rites of ordination and confirmation. All other episcopal duties, such, for instance, as that of an annual visitation of all the parishes within the peculiar, were reserved to the chapter. But it had certain powers with respect to ordination even, for in 1248 the chapter laid down the conditions for the selection of those who should be ordained by the authority of the church, a spiritual examination before the canons being one of the conditions. No doubt the church gained much pecuniary benefit also from the general synods, since all the fees usually paid to the ordinary, such as fees for dispensations, faculties, licences, presentments, and so forth, would be received by the chapter. All this explains what is meant when we read that Thomas II. of York granted the prebends of Southwell exemption from all episcopal customs and exaction in churches and lands; and again, when we are told that the churches of the prebends and of the lands belonging to the canons in common were exempt from all episcopal jurisdiction and custom. Mark, however, it is the prebends, the separate prebendal estates, not the prebendaries who were the owners thereof, who were thus exempt. Although the arch-

bishops intrusted all this power to the canons, and though the
chapter had, in theory at any rate, free exercise of this
authority in its own church as in every other church in the
jurisdiction, yet the archbishops by no means released the
canons themselves from their own influence and authority.
They were not only the patrons of the college, which means,
of course, that the prebends were in their gift, but they were
also its visitors; and as such, from time to time, they granted
indulgences, decided appeals, and enacted statutes for its
well-being, for the correction of abuses, and the good conduct of
matters relating to the church; and in one case at least heavy
punishment was threatened in the event of non-compliance.
The popes, of course, intermeddled here as they did everywhere
and for a time almost wholly over-rode the authority of
the archbishops. Their policy, however, was to protect the
interests of the college in every way. Indulgences for varying periods were granted to the canons and their tenants and
parishioners by many successive occupants of the papal see.
Appeals to Rome relative to disputes between the prebendaries
and others were always decided in favour of the former.
More than one instrument to that effect was granted by Urban
III. (1184-1187), while bulls demanding the restoration of
certain lands and benefices withheld from the chapter were
issued by Innocent III. (1194-1216), under whom the power
of the papal see reached its highest point. And there are
bulls from time to time confirming to the chapter and prebendaries their ancient privileges and customs, which are almost
invariably notified as having been originally granted them by
the archbishops in accordance with the customs and privileges
enjoyed by the church and canons of York Perhaps the
most remarkable of these is a bull of Alexander III., dated
1171, which has helped us much in matters we have herein
discussed. This bull grants the prebendaries power to excom-
municate any of their parishioners who may do them injury
in their lands, houses, or church. But of course the wide-
spread evils of the *imperium in imperio* affected the Jurisdiction of Southwell in the same degree as it affected the
country at large. The evil that most nearly affected it perhaps
was that which led up to the famous "Statute of Provisors"
passed in the reign of Edward III. Not only did the popes
usurp the patronage of vacant preferments, but, by means of
provisions or expective graces, they appointed successors to

preferments before they became vacant, receiving from the creatures of their appointment one, two, and sometimes three years' incomes of the benefices in return. It is needless to say that the appointments they made were almost always those of hungry foreigners. Discontent and disturbances consequently prevailed among the lay patrons; and we read how Sir Robert Thwinge, a Yorkshire knight, holding patronage in the time of Gregory IX., with about eighty others, raised an agitation against the system in that county, seized the persons of the foreign intruders, and even murdered the pope's envoys. If full lists of the canons of Southwell during a part of the 13th and 14th centuries were forthcoming, we should see that a great number of them bore Italian names;* and we have evidence that their prebendal houses and estates were allowed to go to rack and ruin while they enjoyed their incomes abroad. A large amount of money was thus taken out of the county, causing, doubtless, untold hardships to the tenants of the estates, while the morals and condition of society in general suffered from the absence of those who ought to have been its leaders. Dismissing, however, these foreign interlopers and their patrons from our minds, let us pass on to consider the position which the archbishops and our native canons held in the county during the middle ages.

The temporal possessions of the archbishops at Southwell date from the reign of Edwy, who gave to his favourite, Oskytel. *XX mansas ad Suthwellam*.† Domesday Book and other authorities allow us to fix the limits within which they exercised their manorial rights from Norman times onward. The Barony, or, as it is more often called, the Manor of Southwell, extended from Fountain Dale, beyond Blidworth in Sherwood Forest, right to a point some three miles east of Southwell. This strip of country—the middle part of Thurgarton Hundred—formed the basis of the two jurisdictions of Southwell: first the Peculiar, which is the ecclesiastic jurisdiction already alluded to; and secondly the Liberty or Soke. This Liberty was one of those great baronial jurisdictions which freed their inhabitants from attendance at the hundred-court, in which the sheriff of the county presided. In fact

---

* I am told that in Milan Cathedral may be seen a memorial of one who is described as "Cardinal of Rome and Canon of Southwell, England."

† An estate of some 2,000 or 2,500 acres.

it is sometimes regarded as a separate hundred, called Southwell wapentake or hundred. The archbishop was therefore
a great feudal lord, and held court-baron twice a year, enjoy-
ing all the rights and profits which would otherwise have
gone to the crown through the sheriff. The Liberty in time
grew in extent by the addition of certain detached portions
of other hundreds, and at the present day the Liberty of
Southwell and Scrooby forms one of the divisions of the
county for judicial purposes. The Lord-Lieutenant nominates
the Justices of the Peace, but until recently they were nominated
by the archbishop, who by his steward held court-baron also:
relics of his ancient rights. The Peculiar, also, was gradually
increased by the formation of new prebends in other parts of
the county. When it became fixed in extent it included
twenty-four parishes and twenty-eight churches, and it was
in these that the chapter exercised episcopal functions as
ordinary. A classified list is given in a note.* The prebendaries must have been men of great power and position in the
county: they were like feudal lords holding their fiefs direct
from the archbishop, and moreover they obtained great privileges by the special chartas granted to them by the early
Norman kings and confirmed by their successors almost without exception. We read that they enjoyed "view of *frank-
pledge*" of all their tenants, and received "the amercements
"of their tenants, and fines for all such offences as they had
"been guilty of." They were also exempt from all tolls and
duties, such as pontage, "from suits of counties, hundreds,
"and wapentakes, and from all gelds, such as Dane-geld;"

---

* THURGARTON WAPENTAKE OR HUNDRED.

Within the Manor of Southwell.

Southwell.	Edingley.	Upton.
Halam.	Kirklington.	Morton.
Farnsfield.	Halloughton.	Bleasby.
		Blidworth (10).

Without the Manor.

Woodborough.	N. Muskham (with Holme).
Calverton.	S. Muskham.
Oxton.	Norwell (cum Carlton).
	Caunton (17).

BINGHAM WAPENTAKE.
Cropwell Bishop (18).

BASSETLAW WAPENTAKE.

Beckingham.	N. Leverton.	Dunham (cum Ragnall).
S. Wheatley.	Rampton.	Eaton (24).

and they were allowed to have their courts of justice with
sac and soc, and the return of writs, and so on. All this
means that in each township in their prebends the prebendaries held their courts with complete liberty of jurisdiction,
both civil and criminal; and their tenants by attendance at
these courts were freed from attendance at the popular courts
of the hundred and shire administered by the sheriff in the
sheriff's *tourn* or round.* The fines and other profits arising
therefrom must have been very considerable. Frank-pledge
was the police system used in early times. Ten men, forming
a tithing, were pledged as surety for the keeping of the peace
by each member of their tithing. View of frank-pledge was
taken in the hundred and manorial courts-leet in the sheriff's
tourn. But the prebendaries held their own courts-leet for this
purpose twice a year in each township without the presence of
the sheriff since they had the right of *sac and soc* or liberty of
jurisdiction. How far the manorial courts-baron and the courts-
leet were associated together, or whether they were kept separate, I do not know. Of course the legal reforms of Henry II.
and the institution of the Itinerant Justices tended to deprive
these courts of jurisdiction in criminal cases; but it was a
long time before the powers of criminal administration were
wholly wrested from these private courts. In the 14th century it was a common thing for the sheriffs to infringe upon
the rights of liberties and manors which were by right exempt
from their jurisdiction, to the loss of the lords of the manors.
The frequent occurrence of pleas before the King at Westminster, as well as before the Justices in Eyre in the reigns of
Edward III. and Richard II., illustrates this in the case of
the prebends of Southwell, but in each case it appears the
canons came off victorious and a writ of allowance follows.
There is extant in the Registrum Album a charter of Henry
I. confirming to the canons of S. Peter of York their ancient
privileges. This quaint document is worthy of quotation,
because we find the privileges of the canons of Southwell so
often affirmed to be the same as those enjoyed by the canons
of York. The charter was granted on account of a complaint
made to the king in 1106 that the rights of the canons were
much infringed by the sheriff of the county. The commission
appointed to inquire into the matter testified "that all the

---

* On the whole subject of the judicial administration see Professor
Stubbs' *Constitutional History of England.*

B

"land belonging to the prebends of the church of S. Peter
"was so quiet and free, that neither the king's officer nor any
"other could have law nor take a distress there till the canon
"of that prebend was first inquired: and, if he refused, the
"dean should set a day and do right at the church door.
"And if any person whatsoever shall detain any man, though
"guilty, and convict of any crime whatever, from within the
"porch, he shall always be adjudged to make amends by six
"hundredths; if from within the church, by twelve; if from
"within the choir, by eighteen: every hundredth containing
"six pounds, and for every or any of the said faults shall be
"enjoined penance as for sacrilege. But if any should be so
"mad or instigated by the devil as to presume to take one
"from the stone-chair by the altar, which the English call
"*frithstol*, that is, the chair of peace, for so wicked a sacrilege
"no judgment or sum of money can atone." Then follows
an enumeration of the privileges of *sac and soc* and the like.*

The possession of large estates tended to secularise the lives
of the canons of Southwell. Their social influence among the
people as feudal lords was doubtless greater than their spiritual
influence as priests of Southwell. They owned each a large
residence house in Southwell, and doubtless they had mansions
upon their prebendal estates also. They were great huntsmen,
keeping their pack of hounds and owning great forest rights.
King Stephen, by a precept dated at York, directed to William
Peverell and the sheriff of Notts. and his ministers, commanded "that the canons of S. Mary of Suwell should have
"the woods of their prebends in their own hands and custody,
"and thence take what they should need, as in King Henry's
"time, and that his foresters be forbidden to take or sell any-

---

* The right of sanctuary, which freed a criminal from all except
ecclesiastical punishment, played an important part in the middle
ages in preventing the excesses of private revenge, though of course
it was often abused Mr. Parker describes the *frithstool* or *freedstool*
as a "seat or chair placed near the altar in some ancient churches, the
"last and most sacred refuge for those who claimed the privilege of
"sanctuary within them, and for violation of which the severest
"punishment was decreed." Frithstools still exist at Hexham and
Beverley. According to Spelman the last-named had this inscription:
"Hic sedes lapidea *freedstoll* dicitur, i.e. pacis cathedra, ad quam
"reus fugiendo perveniens omnimodam habet securitatem." We are
reminded of Joab and Adonijah, and "the horns of the altar."—Add.
MSS. 4292 in Brit. Mus. is a quaint register of persons who sought
refuge at Beverley.

"thing there." The whole of the western part of the liberty, that part in which Blidworth is situated, was included in the perambulations of the Royal Forest of Sherwood.

It may be well at this point to review briefly the position which the college held in the middle ages. I. The church, being the mother church of the county, held much the same high position therein as our cathedrals now hold in their respective dioceses. The chapter, however, derived certain additional privileges therefrom, more particularly pecuniary ones. II. The jurisdiction of the chapter, acting as ordinary, extended only over a more limited area, called the Peculiar, and was purely spiritual. III. But the chapter and individual prebendaries gained in Norman times many temporal judicial powers, partly in virtue of their fiefs as territorial lords, and partly from the special royal chartas granted to them. These included the right of holding courts, whether courts-baron or courts-leet, to which all their tenants should repair, of deciding pleas therein, of inflicting punishment upon criminals, of taking tolls upon the sales of goods, and of enacting the bye-laws which ruled the townships. IV. And lastly we must mention the illegal judicial powers which the church every-where usurped in the 12th and 13th centuries under the influence and guidance of the papal see. It claimed for its members right of jurisdiction in all cases, civil and criminal, in which any clerk was concerned, which, together with the right of sanctuary, tended to place almost the whole adminis-tration of justice in its hands. I need scarcely remind the reader of the Constitutions of Clarendon and the efforts of Henry II. to reform this abuse, which failed however at first to have much effect. The bull of Alexander III. shews that the canons of Southwell assumed certain powers in connection with this system, but the extent of their powers from other sources forbids us to think they took any prominent share in upholding the usurpation.

Before considering the constitution of the college we have to make a few historical notes. Of the sixteen prebends as many as ten had been formed by the time of the Norman Conquest or very shortly after:

Norwell Overall.	Oxton prima pars.
Norwell Palishall.	Oxton altera pars.
Norwell tertia pars.	North Muskham.
Normanton.	South Muskham.
Woodborough.	Sacrista.

The names of the remaining six, with the particulars of their foundations, are as follows:

Dunham : founded by Abp. Thurstan ; *tempus* Henry I.

Beckingham : by the same.

Halloughton, or the Lay Prebend : by Abp. Roger ; *tempus* Henry II.

Rampton : by Pavia Maluvel, daughter of Nigellus de Rampton, with consent of her son Robert ; *tempus* John.

Eaton : by Abp. John Romanus ; in the year 1289.

Leverton : formed by a division of the prebend of Beckingham in 1291.

Thurstan, the hero of the battle of the Standard and founder of the see of Carlisle, shewed a decided preference for the stricter discipline of the monastic foundations. The importance of the mother church of Southwell was specially marked therefore by his founding two prebends. Abp. Roger de Pont L'Eveque was chiefly remarkable for the part he took with Henry II against Thomas à Becket, and for his resistance to the Archbishops of Canterbury, who claimed the submission and dependence of the see of York to that of Canterbury. The reigns of Richard I. and John his brother were times of unrest and anxiety for the northern province. How far the canons of Southwell supported their archbishop in his quarrels with the king, resisting his extortionate demands, I cannot say, but they cannot have stood by as calm observers. Abp Geoffrey Plantagenet, natural son of Henry II., was himself perhaps the very worst man who ever filled the see. Before his election in 1191 the see was vacant for ten years, and again for other nine years on his retirement to Normandy in 1203.

The episcopate of his successor, Walter de Gray, 1216-1255, was an important epoch in the history of the diocese at large, and of Southwell Minster in particular Walter, besides being a leading statesman and trusted counsellor of Henry III., shewed himself a strong ecclesiastical ruler, energetic in the reform and organization of his diocese. He revived the meetings of the clergy in the diocesan synods, which had fallen somewhat into abeyance; reorganized the ruri-decanal chapters; and helped to bring together the northern and southern provinces in convocation. The share that the general clergy took in managing the affairs of the diocese is the keynote of his system. The canons of S. Peter formed his council and shared with him his labours; and there is evidence that he frequently consulted the chapters of the other mother churches of the diocese also, of Southwell, Ripon, and Beverley.*

He devoted much attention, too, to the improvement of the fabric of these churches. The west front of Ripon is said to be his work. Under him, John Romanus, subdean, began the rebuilding of York Minster in the north transept. And, which is more to the point, the small Norman choir of Southwell Minster was replaced by one more suited to its needs and position, for "the consummation" of which he granted an indulgence of thirty days' pardon to all who should contribute towards the funds of the fabric. He is said to have given to "his church of Southwell a collection of very wise statutes for the government of the body." These I have not seen.

An MS. preserved among the chapter records, entitled *The Statutes*,† contains statutes granted by three of the archbishops as well as other important matter, from which much of our information is drawn:

Charta of Abp. Walter Giffard, dated 1274.
Charta of Abp. John Romanus, 1294.
Statutes of Thomas de Corbridge, 1302.

John Romanus is worthy of some notice. In 1291 he laid the foundation of the beautiful nave of York Minster. One striking similarity in the architecture of this building to a peculiar feature in the earlier choir of Southwell seems to warrant the conclusion that it is a copy. And the exact similarity in plan of Southwell chapter house, built in the time of this prelate, to the peculiar chapter-house of York, built about the same time, is another link in the chain of connection between the two minsters, and proves the common influence of Abp. John.

Now we come to the consideration of the constitution of the college. A few historical notices will creep in to complete the sketch, as well as some account of the customs of the church. The following table presents itself:

    I. The Archbishop: Patron and Visitor.
    II. The Prebendaries: The Chapter.
    III. The Vicars Choral.
    IV. The Chantry Priests.
    V. The Choristers.

---

* Mr. Ormsby's *York*. † Mr. Dimock says this was compiled probably towards the end of Queen Elizabeth's reign.

I. Much has already been said of the archbishop and his relation to the. college, but I must add a few words to guard against any misunderstanding. He was something more than the mere patron and visitor of later times. The archbishops had founded the college; they had given much of their own property to endow it; they had their palace within the minster precincts and their throne in the minster itself; and some of them at least made frequent use of both. The connection was of the closest nature: they guided the destinies of the college by their official statutes and by their personal influence, while the chapter or its representatives, forming a part of their council, helped them in the affairs of the diocese. This may be an ideal conception of their mutual relations, but in some cases at least it was borne out in practice.

II. It was in the 13th century that the constitution of our secular cathedrals and colleges assumed a settled form. The *quattuor personæ* or four great officers, the dean, precentor, chancellor, and treasurer, were the mainspring of law and order. Southwell, however, presents one or two striking peculiarities in its constitution. To begin with, there was no fixed president of the chapter. The dean is usually the president, but at Southwell there was no dean, as was the case at both S. David's and Llandaff. At S. David's the precentor was president, and at Llandaff the archdeacon. There was no archdeacon of Southwell, his duties, as far as the peculiar was concerned, being performed by one of the canons selected annually for the purpose, who, taking with him one of the vicars and the registrar of the chapter, made a visitation of all the churches of the prebends to inspect the morals, behaviour, and condition of the clergy and tenants. The archdeaconry of Nottingham was founded in the 12th century, but was attached to York without any jurisdiction in the peculiar of Southwell. Nor can I find any mention of a precentor of Southwell. This was a very important officer in cathedral churches, since the whole management of the service and conduct of the choir were in his hands; but it was a common arrangement in simply collegiate churches for the dean to undertake the duties of the office, the purely musical part of it being entrusted by him to *rectores chori* or leaders of the choir. Such an arrangement existed in the collegiate churches of Astley and Chester-le-Street. At Southwell the duties of both dean and precentor must have been undertaken by the canon residentiary, a position filled by the canons in

turn, each for some fixed period,* probably three months.
Such a system can have had little or nothing to recommend
it, nevertheless it was followed by the prebendaries even of
later times. The college seems to have never been famous for
its internal organization, notwithstanding the solicitude of the
early archbishops, Walter Gray and John Romanus, the
master-minds of the see of York in the 13th century, for its
general welfare and good government. Though it lacked dean
and precentor, yet Southwell had its chancellor and treasurer.
The jurisdiction of the chancellor, strange to say, stretched
beyond the limits of the peculiar over the whole county of
Nottingham. This officer, who is not to be confounded with
the modern chancellor of the diocese, had "to instruct the
"yoonger sort of cannons," as Godwin tells us. But he had
more to do than this: he was the great educational officer of
the county, the inspector of schools, so to speak. He was
also the librarian, and had care of the church literature. The
prebend of Normanton was attached to the chancellorship, as
well as nearly one-half of the pentecostal offerings. A further
fraction of one-tenth of the pentecostals was given to the
treasurer, who at Southwell was called the sacristan, a name
which gave the name of Sacrista to the prebend held by this
officer. The business of the treasurer in a collegiate church
was "to look to the ornaments of the church," namely the
vestments, church plate, and so forth; he was also master of
the fabric. In the capitular statutes of 1248 mention is
made of a *Custos Fabricæ*, who was to render an account of
all his receipts once every year to two canons resident, and
was to have some canon or vicar of the church associated with
him to bear witness to his receipts. I have no doubt that
reference is here made to the sacristan. At York the sacristan
was guardian of the fabric. He also had the oversight of the
church servants, having under him a sub-treasurer, two clerks
of the vestry, and three sacrists, besides others. John
Romanus enacted that a sacrist should lie within the church
at Southwell, to be at hand to ring the bells at the right time.
Our word *sexton*, in middle English *sextain*, is only a shorten-
ing of sacristan. The following is a note from the note-book

---

* As appears from an *item* in the Charta of Abp. John Roma:
"Caveant Residentiarii Canonici quod nullus succedens alii residendo
"mandatum scribat illi contrarium quod per præcedentem suum
"Residentem Canonicum nomine Capituli emanavit," etc.

of Sir R. Kaye, dean of Lincoln and prebendary of Southwell, obiit 1809 : "The tennant [of the sacristan's prebendal house "and lands, leased in 1571] is to find bread and wine for the "communion from time to time to be ministred and spent in "the collegiate church of Southwell, and also bell ropes and "washing of the church cloths, and be at such like necessary "expenses as heretofore used to be incumbent upon the "sacristan prebendary." Thus much of the higher offices in the church : I do not know the dates of their foundation.

The property of the chapter was of two kinds. First there were the prebends, the separate endowments enjoyed by the individual prebendaries; then there were also certain lands enjoyed by the canons in common as a capitular body. This latter kind of property was called the *communia*. Beides these we must mention certain lands bequeathed by various bene-factors and set apart for the actual expenses of the fabric, which were therefore called *our lady's lands*. All other expenses connected with the church, excepting some specified ones defrayed by the sacristan, were paid out of the communia. This, however does not include the salaries of the vicars and chantry priests, which we shall treat of later on. The residue of the communia was, at the feast of pentecost in each year, equally divided among such of the canons who had kept three months' residence, either continuous or divided into two parts. A canon might, however, with the leave of his brothers resident, absent himself during his residence if urgent business made it necessary, but he had to make up the lost time before the close of the year or he lost his dividend. Before the division took place, certain other deductions were made in favour of individual canons. For attendance at a "matins of nine lections" a canon received the sum of threepence, and sixpence for a "double festival." These rules, laid down by Abp. Walter Giffard in 1274, giving certain pecuniary advan-tages to the canons who kept residence, seem to imply that they had become lax in the performance of their duties, choosing rather a life of ease and enjoyment on their separate estates, or of lucrative employment elsewhere. In fact we more than once meet with some such expression as *casu con-tingente nullo canonico tunc residente* about this time : it was essentially an age of non-residence and pluralities. Other bribes to residence were now offered to the prebendaries: the same archbishop gave the church of Rolleston for the benefit of the canons resident; John Romanus, too, increased the fund for their daily commons. This no doubt caused a general desire to rush into residence, so much so that the canons already in residence cast about them for means to prevent the others from coming in to enjoy the advantages that would accrue to them therefrom, whereby the annual dividends would be sensibly lessened. Hence we find the canons resident in 1335 making a rule that no one holding a "litigious prebend" should be admitted to residence, or even be allowed to take any part in the councils or acts of the chapter, until he obtained "peaceful possession."* Nor could any canon protest† residence until he had held peaceful possession of his prebend for the space of a whole year. The administration of the communia was entrusted to two officers called *custodes generales communiæ canonicorum.* It is doubtful whether they were themselves canons. The statute of 1329, which provides for their election, merely says that those chosen should be "faithful and fit" for the office. It seems to me the office was much like that of the ancient provost who had charge of the temporalities of a collegiate church, but often without a vote in chapter or stall in choir. The same statute enacts that there should be three chests, kept under three locks (each), the keys of the same to be in the keeping of the two guardians of the communia with the sacristan. The first was to contain the title-deeds of the church and all moneys received; in the second were to be placed the jewels *(jocalia)* and relics of the church; in the third the books of the community, *i.e.* the chapter records and statutes, to which no one should be allowed access without proper caution. A prebendary was supposed to institute a perpetual vicar into each of the parish churches of his prebend. Some of the canons failed to do this, preferring to hold the cures in their own hands, or perhaps leaving them unadministered altogether, as would be the case with the foreign canons. This omission called forth rebuke from John Romanus in 1294.

* On the whole subject of Residence see Mr. E. A. Freeman's *Wells.*

† A newly-elected Canon, before entering upon residence, had to make public "protestation and premonition" of his intention on three separate occasions, within the octave of the Feast of S. Michael, in Chapter at the *Preciosa,* before the Canon Resident, or, there being no Canon in Residence, before the Custodes or Guardians of the Chapter. *Statutes* of 1302. The Preciosa was an anthem, "Precious in the sight of the Lord, etc," sung immediately after the reading of the Martyrology and before that of the Tabula or weekly roll of services and officiating clergy.—Walcott's *Cathedralia.*

III. The Vicars of the prebendaries in the collegiate church itself were at once their assistants and their deputies. The frequent absence of the canons from Southwell made it necessary for them to have their duties in choir fulfilled by deputy, while their want in many cases of any practical knowledge of church music rendered them unable without assistance to perform them thoroughly when present. Each canon therefore appointed his own vicar, paying him the sum of £3 annually. The appointment was made in favour of any *clericus* who had been in the service of a canon, and it was subject to the approval of the chapter. Thus there were sixteen vicars in all, each occupying in choir the seat below the stall of his canon. This is a feature common to constitutions of all the more important collegiate churches. As in other churches, the vicars of Southwell at an early date were formed into a separate college, with corporate rights and endowments, and with their own collegiate buildings. The date of the foundation of the college of vicars choral, as they are called later on, is fixed with some degree of certainty only by inference. Archbishop Walter Gray, whose powers of organization have already been spoken of, incorporated the vicars of York about 1240 or 1241. In the Southwell statutes of 1248 the vicars are spoken of as a *fraternity*, with power to elect a custos of their communia or common property, and bound *corporali sacramento*, by an oath, that is, taken by each one of them at his institution into office. The inference is that the vicars of Southwell also were incorporated by Walter Gray between the years 1240 and 1248. According to Thoroton their seal, with the inscription *Commune Sigillum Vicariorum Suuel*, was affixed to a deed bearing date 1262. Before their incorporation the vicars probably lived in the houses of their respective *masters*. From this time, however, they inhabited a common dwelling situated on the east side of the brook called Bullivant's Dyke. In the course of a century or so this building fell into a ruinous state, so that they had to find separate lodgings in different parts of the town. This giving rise to certain scandals, Richard de Chesterfield, in the year 1379, with the leave of the pope and archbishop, built a quadrangular college for them at his own cost on the site occupied by the present vicars' court. The living rooms extended along three sides of the quadrangle, the college hall occupying the fourth or eastern side where the residence house now stands. In this hall the canons, vicars, and other ministers of the church received their commons or daily meals. The proceeds from their corporate estates was divided yearly among the vicars, and in addition each one received from his *master* a salary of sixty shillings, as we have seen, as well as two shillings for celebrating mass for their dead brethren. A fine of one penny for each occasion of absence went to swell the communia before division took place, and a fine of two shillings for breaking their oath was similarly applied. In the year 1373 all their separate estates were conveyed "for their benefit," it is said, to the chapter. What advantages they gained from the conveyance do not appear. It is very possible, however, that in return the chapter allowed the number of vicars to be considerably reduced. This arrangement suited both parties. The remaining vicars would receive from the chapter larger stipends than they had taken at the division of their communia among the full number of sixteen vicars   The chapter would be far from losers from a monetary point of view from the transaction, while it would regain the influence and ascendancy over the vicars which their corporate rights must to some extent have deprived it of. It is not unlikely that the great change in the constitution of the body of vicars marked by their yielding up their property into the hands of the chapter was accompanied by a further change in their numbers. About the time of the reformation there seem to have been even less than six vicars. Mr. Dickenson's arguments that the reduction in their numbers took place at the time of their incorporation have no foundation in fact, and the date we have assigned, though unsupported by documentary evidence, is a much more likely one.

IV. The Chantry Priests next come under notice. When in the 13th century the foundation of large religious communities for the most part ceased, men of means began to expend their wealth in the erection of chantry chapels in the aisles and transepts of their churches. These chapels were generally separated off by parcloses of wood and beautifully painted; sometimes they took the form of stone-work additions to the east ends of the aisles and transepts. They contained altars to which priests, supported by plentiful endowments, were attached, who said, daily or otherwise, private mass for the souls of the founders living or dead, or for such persons as were specified in the conditions of the foundation. The tombs of the founders were usually placed within them, and the sites of the altars, demolished at the reformation, is in

many cases marked at the present day by the piscinas and
aumbries which were suffered to remain in the walls. These
private chapels were very numerous, not only in our cathedrals
and abbeys, but also in many of our parochial churches, and
the old altar-slabs may often still be seen in the floorings,
marked with the five crosses symbolic of the five wounds
of our crucified Saviour:

Vulnera quinque Dei sint medicina mei.

Prayer for the faithful departed was a very early practice of
the Christian church. The motives which prompted it, pure
and praiseworthy in themselves, were gradually alloyed by
superstition and false doctrine. The *missa pro defunctis*, or
celebration of mass for the deliverance of the soul from the
pains of hell, was the natural outcome of the doctrine of
purgatory and grew with it. The celebrating priest was the
only recipient of the mystical elements, and often the only
other person present was the assisting acolyte. The chantry-
chapels were dedicated to some saint or saints. In Southwell
Minster there were nine such:

S. John the Baptist.	S. Nicholas.
S. John the Evangelist.	S. Cuthbert.
S. Peter.	S. Michael.
S. Stephen.	S. Mary Magdalene.
S. Thomas the Martyr or Thomas à Becket.	

The number of masses, however, was thirteen, certain altars
being served by more than one priest: four for the living,
eight for the dead, and one for the Blessed Virgin Mary.
Some few of our larger churches dedicated to the Virgin seem
to have had no chapel specially dedicated to her. Thus
Southwell is without a lady-chapel.

The thirteen chantry priests, like the vicars, formed a
separate community, owned common property, and lived
together in *The Chauntry*, which stood in the N.W. corner
of the church-yard, on the ground now occupied by the new
buildings of the collegiate school. Those were days when every
ecclesiastical body endeavoured to gain corporate independ-
ence and exemption from any superior jurisdiction. When
the doctrine of purgatory was renounced at the reformation
their existence was swept away. They had other duties in
the church besides the celebration of private masses. They
had to "follow the choir" with the vicars, and were subject
to the same fines for non-attendance and to the same general

rules of discipline. Speaking of discipline, the conduct of the vicars of Southwell and other subordinate ministers of the church, like that of their brethren of York, seems to been no credit to the church. They were frequenters of taverns, shows, and other low meetings, leading in fact a generally loose life.* The more heinous offences were punishable with suspension, and on a third conviction with expulsion. Moreover they had to be reproved by the archbishop for talking and laughing in choir. If one were convicted for swearing within the church he had to pay a fine of two shillings to the fabric, or be subjected to *two disciplines*, an expression which seems to denote corporal punishment, in chapter and before his fellows. A fine of one shilling was imposed in a case of swearing outside the church; or, if the canon resident thought fit, the offender had to go about on a certain Sunday carrying on his back, tied round his neck, an old leathern knapsack†—an ancient custom of the church. The standard of morality among the clergy was a low one, but the means adopted for raising it are certainly amusing.

V. There is nothing to say about the choristers, except that they were a distinct body in the early constitution, as is evident from the fact that John Romanus granted the rectory of Barneby, near Newark, to the chapter for their support. We may take this opportunity of saying a few words about the singing-men. It must be remembered that no laymen were admitted to office in the church in early times. The services of the church were performed entirely by clerks in orders,‡ with the help of chorister-boys only. Thus the singing-men were a later institution, but the date of their coming into being cannot be fixed even approximately. They were evidently well established when Queen Elizabeth granted her statutes to the church, and may have been so long before her reign. It may be that they were appointed when the number of vicars was reduced, whenever that was. It is more likely, however, that they were not wanted until the suppression of the chantries by Edward VI. withdrew the help of the

---

* Amoveantur mulieres a domibus Vicariorum (personis conjunctis quae careant omni suspicione exceptis) sub poena subtractionis stipendii et privationis officiorum et beneficiorum suorum si eorum pertinacia ita exposcat.—Abp. John Romanus, 1294.

† *Bulgewarium;* from the Gallic word *Bulga*, whence *Bougette.*

‡ Et quod *Clerici Cantaturi* in choro inspiciant tabulam, et provideant versus suos, et ea quae sint canenda, et quod cantent sine libro.

chantry priests. But this is mere conjecture; the point to notice is that the singing-men, whenever they came into existence, did not form a part of the constituted body attached to the church, but were mere stipendiaries, having no corporate rights like the lay-vicars of many of our cathedrals of the old foundation,* of Wells for instance, where the vicars choral at some period before the reformation were divided into priest-vicars and lay-vicars, still forming one corporate body and continuing to do so down to the present day. At York and Hereford likewise the office of vicar choral has never been filled by laymen, the singing-men or lay-clerks being mere stipendiaries in the pay of the chapter, as is the case at cathedrals of the new foundation.†

In the foregoing sketch I have endeavoured to trace in a general and comprehensive way the origin and development of the position which the college of Southwell held in the middle ages. Its particular history illustrates the history of the church at large. The two great causes of the church's power as a civil and political engine were, first, the monopoly of learning enjoyed by the monks and the higher secular clergy; and secondly, its great landed wealth. Long before the actual reformation of the church came about, the pedestal on which these two influences had placed it was slowly and surely being undermined. The beginning of the long struggle against the one is marked by the Constitutions of Clarendon and the endeavour to narrow the limits of ecclesiastical jurisdiction, while the Statute of Mortmain shews a growing sense of fear of the power which lay in the possession of large landed

---

* The cathedrals of the old foundation are those which, being served by secular canons, were not suppressed by Henry VIII.: Wells, Salisbury, Exeter, York, London, Lincoln, Lichfield, Hereford, Chichester, and the four of Wales. The cathedrals of the new foundation are those which, being served by monks, were dissolved along with the other monasteries, and refounded sooner or later as chapters of secular canons: Winchester, Canterbury, Rochester, Norwich, Worcester, Durham, Ely, and Carlisle; together with the churches which were made cathedral for the first time by Henry VIII.: Oxford, Peterborough, Chester, Gloucester and Bristol, and Westminster which lost its bishop and became collegiate in the next reign; and in our own time Ripon and Manchester, S. Albans and Truro, and Liverpool and Newcastle, to which Southwell and Wakefield will soon be added.—See Mr. Freeman's *Wells.*

† Here we may add a list of existing collegiate chapters: Westminster, Windsor, Heytesbury, Middleham, and S. Katharine's Hospital.

estates. The disclosure by Wiclif and his followers of the evil effects of a system which made the clergy forget their spiritual functions in fulfilling their worldly and political duties, and which allowed such a glaring abuse as the "benefit of clergy" to exist, prepared the way for the New Learning which was destined to reform church doctrine; and the severity of the measures found necessary to repress the tenets of Lollardism is a sure sign of the growth of that independent thought among the uneducated classes which was soon to be cultivated by the invention of printing and the general revival of literature and learning. The reformation in England was certainly hurried on by causes purely political, but the reform of doctrine followed closely upon the proclamation of the Royal Supremacy, and when the church emerged from the troubles of the 16th century, not its doctrine only, but its whole system had gone through the process of purification, and the power that was left it was no longer civil and political but rather social and spiritual.

The change might be traced in the history of the college of Southwell. In following its varying fortunes in the period of the reformation it will be necessary to give little more than a bare statement of the changes through which it passed. In 1540 the college ceased to exist by the voluntary surrender of its property to King Henry VIII.* We have not far to go to seek the reasons. The suppression of the lesser monasteries, begun by Wolsey and completed by Cromwell in 1536, was doubtless prompted by good political reasons. But Henry's appetite for the church's wealth was whetted thereby, and Cromwell, disappointed perhaps that parliament had refused to sanction the dissolution of the larger abbeys also, was not a man to stick at trifles. What he could not effect by legal measures he gained by extortion and cruelty. The whole monastic body was driven to despair by the severity and inso- lence of the commissioners sent to carry out the act of '36, and they saw their end was near. Those abbots who did not surrender their monasteries voluntarily were appointed by the vicar-general to be "tried and executed," and their estates confiscated to the crown. The illegal plundering already almost completed was confirmed by act of parliament in '39, and the panic immediately spread to all ecclesiastical bodies throughout the kingdom. It was this fear that dictated to

---

* Rym. Fœd. xiv. 674.

the prebendaries of Southwell the advisability of anticipating further robbery by surrendering their college in '40 to the King of their own accord.* It seems to have been good policy on their part, for the very next year saw it refounded and re-endowed at the request of Archbishop Cranmer, himself a Nottinghamshire man.† As a salve to his conscience Henry proposed to erect fifteen new sees out of the proceeds of the plunder, Southwell being one of them. But his intention was realised in only six cases, and the bishopric of Southwell seems never to have been endowed,‡ though Dr. Cox,§ one of the prebendaries, was nominated to fill it. In the meantime began the "systematic picking and stealing" of church goods which was still more characteristic of the next reign, and Southwell, as we shall see, suffered sadly.

It was not till 1541, the first year of Edward VI., that the climax came, when all chantries and colleges were suppressed, with the exception of cathedral chapters, the colleges in the universities, and a few others, some of which we had occasion to mention in the early part of this chapter. Beverley, Southwell, and Ripon fell with the rest, and became simply parish churches. From this time Beverley ceased altogether to be collegiate. The temporalities of Southwell were granted to the Earl of Warwick, afterwards Duke of Northumberland: it has been said that in this way something like one-fifth of the land in the kingdom had by this time passed from the church into the hands of the nobles and gentry. Warwick sold them to one John Beaumont, Master of the Rolls, and

* In 1542, Abp. Lee alienated to the crown the manor of Southwell in exchange for lands belonging to certain dissolved priories. His successor, Holgate, alienated from the see as many as six other manors. They were granted to the see again by Mary in Abp. Heath's episcopate.—State Papers.

† Rot. Act Parl. 33 Henry VIII.

‡ Professor Willis, however, says that Southwell was actually endowed for a time, as well as Dunstable, Shrewsbury, Bodmin, and Colchester. At the same time, it may be, it was proposed to appoint a dean as head of the chapter, which would account for the description of the church given in the edition of the *Monasticon* published in 1716, to the effect that it "had anciently a dean, archdeacon, and other dignitaries."

§ Dr. Cox was tutor to Prince Edward and Dean of Cardinal College, now Christ Church, Oxford, one of "those twins of learning" of Wolsey's creation, of which Cox had been elected fellow in 1525. Under Queen Elizabeth he became Bishop of Ely.

father to Francis Beaumont, Judge of the Common Pleas in 5 Edward VI. From John Beaumont they were again brought to the crown by conveyance or otherwise, and again granted to the Duke of Northumberland.* At the attainder of Northumberland in 1553 they once more passed into the possession of the crown. This was a piece of good fortune for the prebendaries of Southwell, for it enabled. Queen Mary to reinstate them in their former possessions and rights. Her action was immediately due to the personal influence of Abp. Heath, who succeeded the deprived Holgate in '55, but it was entirely consistent with her declared policy. She managed to bring back the church, as far as the marriage of the clergy and the conduct of its public service were concerned, to the condition in which it existed in the earlier years of her father's reign. She wished to go further and restore the church lands which had been alienated from the monasteries, colleges, and guilds, but to this her parliament would not consent, nor could the transfer have been practically effected even had parliament given its consent. It was only some such chance as occurred in the case of Southwell which enabled her to re-establish the college of Ripon, the monastery of Westminster under Abbot Frekenham, and a few other monastic houses. To return to Southwell, of course Mary's grant had practically the effect of restoring the college to its old position, but the restoration was not legal, being in direct opposition to the Act of Suppression, which had not been repealed. On these grounds it was argued,† half a century later, that "the chapter of S. Mary's Church of Southwell is vested in "the crown by statute 1 Edward VI.," enabling James I. in 1604 to make the magnanimous "grant and confirmation to "the chapter of the Collegiate Church of Southwell of the "site and precinct of the church and the possessions belonging "thereto."‡ In the meantime Queen Elizabeth had granted statutes for the government of the college, which is therein spoken of as having been founded by her most illustrious father in evident reference to the act of 1541, but no mention is made of its suppression by Edward VI., nor is the legality or rather illegality of its renewed existence discussed, as is the case in the somewhat similar statutes granted by the Queen to the chapter of Wells.

---

* Thoroton's *Nottinghamshire.*   † State Papers, 1608.

‡ State Papers, 1604.   Add. Ch. 15241, Brit. Mus.

c

The history of this particular church, thus briefly surveyed, serves very well as an illustration of the spoliation of the church at large, and it was only the strong personal influence with the crown of men in high position—first Abp. Cranmer, and afterwards Abp. Heath—which redeemed it from the fate it would otherwise have shared with the monasteries and its fellow colleges. The darkest page in its history is that which tells of the robbery of the church's ornaments, seized by King Henry* for the gratification of his own vanity or to supply means for the attainment of his personal pleasures. We gain our information on this point from the three letters† of Sir Edward North, chancellor of that most iniquitous court, the Court of the Augmentations of the King's Revenues, addressed to his "lovynge Frends the Prebendaries of Suthwell," and also from the Certificate of Chantries and Colleges of 37 Henry VIII.‡ The letters bear no date, but it may be fixed with fair certainty as being slightly anterior to that of the said certificate, perhaps the very same year (1545). They charge the prebendaries with having agreed to make sale of all the plate belonging to the college and to employ the money so raised to their own use and commodity. Besides the sale of the "plate and jewelles, ornaments and other goods "appertayninge to your college to your singular benefitte and "lucre, ye have practysed unlawfullye to sell a chalice and "crosse of gold, garnyshed and sett wyth dyverse kinds of "preceious stones belongyinge to the sayde colledge." Then follows a command to appoint "two of the discreatest Prebendaries ther" to bring the same to Sir Edward North with all convenient diligence that he might *shewe* the same to his Grace, according to his Majesty's pleasure! The third letter contains a similar command "to send unto his Heighnes the "aultar table of sylver and gilte which remaynyth in your "church having the picture of our Ladie and other saynets "in the same, bythands of Mr. Adams, who is one of the "Prebendaries of your colledge, with a just and true inven-"torie of all other parcells of plate and other jewelles and

---

* The church had before this era been despoiled of its goods and chalices by Rufus for his Norman expeditions. See an interesting and exhaustive paper upon this part of our subject in the *Notts. Guardian*, under *Local Notes and Queries*, Nos. 163, 164.

† Printed in App. to Dickenson's *Southwell.*

‡ Preserved in Public Record Office.

"goodes given unto your colledge by the King's Highness at
"the time of the erection of the same." In the inventory
37 of Henry VIII. we read of 1133 ounces of plate, "also other
"and beside a chalis of golde wth a patente, a cross of golde
"wth a fote of golde sette to diverse stones, a tabernacle of
"our ladye of silver and gilte withe ii tables of silver and
"gilte enclosing the same, lately delvned by John Adams,
"clerke, to the Kinge Majesties use unto Sr Edward Northe,
"knight." We cannot blame the prebendaries for their
"unlawfulle practyses" by which they endeavoured to preserve to the church at any rate the value and use of what was
lawfully their own. Nor did they stay their hand at the sale
of the plate, for we find them accused likewise of "sellynge
"and fellynge of woodes, grauntynge annuytes, making of
"leases, and other extraordinarie graunts contrarie to the
"godlie meanynge entended and proposed by the King's
"Majestie" upon their erection. It was the only means by
which they could save their property from the grasping
rapacity of the King, and one adopted very generally throughout the kingdom with the same end in view. At the same
time we cannot think the motives of the "discreat" prebendary, Mr. Adams, whose signature is affixed to the certificate
of 37 Henry VIII., were altogether sincere, when we find
that he retained "ii basens of silver weyinge xlvii oz." as a
reward for the part he took in playing into the King's hands.
There are black sheep in almost every fold, and Mr. Adams
appears to have been the black sheep of Southwell college.
We may be sure the spoiler did not leave much that was
considered to be of any value, and yet a few years later
Edward VI. found something to lay his hands upon. This is
the inventory of the ornaments of the church taken in 6
Edward VI.*

fyrst one chales of sylvere and gyltte wth ye corp'aye.
Item ii candlestykkes of latten and ii ault^r clothes.
It. ii towells ii crewetts of led.
It. one vestment of grene sarsenett wth ye aube.
It. a communyone booke a byble and iii salters.
It. in the steple vii bells with cloke and chyme of the same bells
     and a hand bell.
It. As for the chapell in the burgage Mr. Beamont hathe pullyd
     ytt down to the grownde and we have the bell.
It. one chapell in normanton and one bell p'teyninge to the same.

---

* Pub. Rec. Office.

It. There belongythe to the p'ysohe of Southwell viii chapells or
churchys as morton bleisby halughton farnysfeld edyngley
Halome upton and kyrklyngton the inhabytenntts of the
whyche towns hathe presented as apperythe by their bylls.
It. as for magdalene chapell yt ys sold by the kynge and pullyd
down to the grownde.

The statutes* granted by Queen Elizabeth to the church in
the year 1579 are interesting as being the basis of the system
of internal organization which prevailed until the college
ceased to exist. They are very lengthy, and we shall only
glance at the more important provisions they contain. The
archbishop as metropolitan and visitor is to present the statutes
to the church and enforce the observance of them, wherefore
he is to hold a visitation at least once in every three years.
There is to be always a canon residentiary, who is to act as
president of the chapter and keep such hospitality as his
means will allow. Then an entirely new officer is created,
the Vicar-general, to be elected from time to time by the
canons from their own body. He is invested with the full
power and authority of the chapter to perform as their representative all episcopal functions within the peculiar. His
business seems to have resembled somewhat that of the modern
chancellor of a diocese. The statutes are particular in distinguishing his duties from those of the canon residentiary. All
strictly capitular acts, such as the appointment to vacant
benefices, the installation and induction of new canons, and
the like, were reserved to the chapter or the canon residentiary. The latter had also the management of all matters
relating to the internal organization of the church, the conduct
of its services, and so forth; and the rest of the canons as
well as the other ministers and officers were to render obedience
to him as *Dux et Rector*. Other officers for whom the statutes
make provision are: a registrar, who is to be a public notary
and an apparitor; an auditor, a receiver-general, and a custos
of the fabric; the last two not to be canons of the church.
Then mention is made of some minor officers and servants:
the sacrist—no longer it appears the sacristan prebendary—
who is to keep the ornaments of the church and to walk in
procession before the residentiary, or archbishop if present,

* The MS. entitled *Southwell Statutes* contains a copy of the Elizabeth statutes, and I have seen a second MS. copy in the Lambeth
Library. They may be found printed *in extenso* in the *Monasticon* and
in Dickenson's *Southwell*.

and also before the preacher in choir; a verger, bell-ringer, and door-keeper. The number of vicars choral is fixed at not less than six, there having been in recent times too few for the due celebration of divine service. There are to be six singing-men also. The vicars and singing-men are to take their meals together, with the residentiary if possible, otherwise in some respectable and well-regulated house. A *Magister et Rector Chori* is appointed to teach the choristers and play the organ; also to see to the general welfare of the boys, to give them a liberal education in letters and instruct them in modesty of manners at table. And a school-master *(Ludi-Magister)*, a position filled by one of the vicars choral.* The remaining statutes relate to the oaths to be taken by the different members of the church on their appointment to office; to the custody of the plate, title-deeds, and the common seal of the chapter; to the supervision of the estates of the college and the repairs of the prebendal houses; to the installation of canons, the passing and registration of capitular acts, and the like. They mention one or two customs worth notice perhaps: three theological lectures (or not less than two) were to be delivered every week in the vernacular by a canon appointed by the Abp. or the D. and C. of York. The vicars choral, choristers, and other ministers were to attend them regularly, as well as the school-master and his pupils. And a competent canon was to be appointed by the chapter to explain the Catechism, Apostle's Creed, and the Lord's Prayer in the church every Sunday afternoon.

The statutes require very little comment. Their evident intention was to preserve to the chapter, so far as might be, its ancient powers and privileges; but subsequent history shews that they failed in their object. The failure was due in a great measure to the want of a permanent head to keep the machinery of government in motion. The want of a dean, or some other fixed and permanent president of the chapter, affected the welfare of the college as much in later times as it had done throughout its earlier life. The office of Vicar-general was certainly a perpetual one,

---

* Another of the vicars choral discharged the cure of souls in the parish. The Collegiate Church was also the Parish Church, the benefice being in the patronage of the Prebendary of Normanton. Southwell and Ripon are said to be the only churches which survived the period of the Reformation in their double character of collegiate and parochial churches.

but its influence extended to all the churches of the peculiar alike, and was little felt in the church of Southwell in particular. The duties of the canon residentiary were more akin to those of the deans of our cathedral chapters, but they were performed by the prebendaries in turn. The prebendaries themselves at times failed lamentably in the performance of their duties. The injunctions of Abp. Sharp, issued in 1693, imply that they had given up the practice of preaching in their turns, that they had allowed the divinity lectures to fall into abeyance, and, worse still, that sometimes at least the church was altogether "left destitute of a head or "chief to take care of emergent affairs, and to direct and "govern its inferior members and officers," that, in fact, there was no canon residing. The consequence was that the performance of divine service was left entirely in the hands of the vicars and choir-men, whose carelessness and negligence, we are told, brought scandal upon the church, while the gross living and immorality of some of them more than once called for serious rebuke. The acephalous constitution of the chapter rendered it necessary for the archbishops to interfore more in the affairs of the church than the statutes of Elizabeth intended. We find that whenever any more important change was contemplated by the chapter, the capitular acts were confirmed and put into force by injunctions issued by the archbishops. Some doubt has been entertained as to the legality of the action of Abp. Drummond (1761-1776) in abolishing, *sponte sua*, the time-honoured custom of the annual synod held at Pentecost, which the mayor and council of Nottingham attended in state, as well as representatives of every parish in the county. But this was done with the tacit consent of the chapter, and that the archbishops did not obtain any substantial power in the church is proved by the resistance offered to any reforms they suggested which were opposed to the personal interests of the canons.

But to go back to Queen Elizabeth once more, the statutes were evidently intended to place the college on somewhat the same footing as the cathedrals of the old foundation. To several of these, I believe, Elizabeth granted very similar statutes. Their object was to legalize the state of things which for centuries had been growing up in them by abuse. The number of canons had in many of them become so large that it was impossible for them all, even had they wished it, to keep residence. Thus they had become divided into two sets, residentiary and non-residentiary canons, or, as they are now often wrongly distinguished, canons and prebendaries. At Wells, for instance, out of fifty-two canons not less than six and not more than eight were to be elected residentiaries, keeping some three, some four, months' residence in the year, and they divided the communia amongst themselves, to the exclusion of the remaining members of their body. The number of prebenda- ries at Southwell being much smaller, the chapter in 1579 enacted that four of their body should be elected residentiaries. Three years before, viz. in 1576, the date of the Elizabethan statutes, it had also been enacted that the residentiary for the time being should have the whole dividend with all manner of profits appertaining to the jurisdiction of the collegiate church. "And if any [other] residentiary be disposed to lye "here, he shall pay weekly 3s. 4d.; and for his man 2s.; and "every vicar choral 2s. 3d.; and every singing-man, being "disposed to enter into commons with the residentiary, shall "pay 2s. 2d." By these and similar measures, so contrary to the spirit of the foundation of the college, the prebendaries formally abrogated a great part of their lawful rights, and practically gave the finishing touch in blotting out the *collegiate* character of their church. Had the four canons who were elected residentiaries been residentiaries in fact and not in name only, the affairs of the church might have gone on more smoothly and its services conducted in such a manner as to avoid bringing scandal upon it. But they had each to keep a quarterly residence only, and some of them, as we have seen, failed even to do this. Much less does there seem to have been any "disposition to lye here" on the part of any of the prebendaries who were not of the chosen four. At the end of the 17th century, however, the prebendaries seem to have awaked to a keener sense of their duties, and at their request Abp. Sharp issued his injunctions to the college in 1693. The archbishop directed his attention chiefly to a re-arrange- ment of the vicarage, so that each vicar might be able to have house-room therein. He also made provision for the better government of the college, so that all disorderly practices might be prevented, and also for decent and solemn perform- ance of divine worship in the church. At the same time, in accordance with his injunctions, a change was made in the mode of keeping residence. It was decreed in chapter that for the future the residentiaries be not confined to four, but that all the prebendaries do, according to their respective seniorities, keep a quarterly residence. The church can have gained little by the change, which was merely a falling back to the ancient system. In fact this is the only thing that can be said in its favour, that it restored to the whole body of canons their ancient rights, and made them all take their share in the duties of the church. But the dangers attending a system by which each prebendary came into residence once only in four years, and then stayed no longer than three months, are manifest. Many of them cared little for the time-honoured institution to which they belonged, so long as it gave them some additional wealth and raised their position in the church. Now and then we find one rising above the level of his fellows and correcting some abuse or pushing some reform. Not that the prebendaries of Southwell were one whit more lethargic than the general clergy. They were often pious men, scholars, and gentlemen; but they were infected with the religious torpor which everywhere characterized the church of the 18th century. It was an age of pluralities and spiritual ease, when many a priest lived upon a sinecure or drew his income from a church he seldom or never visited, while populous parishes were growing up in our towns left altogether destitute of spiritual oversight. The following anecdote well illustrates the general situation:—" Oliver and " Watkins wanted to discontinue choral service at Southwell. " Lord Harborough, prebendary, observed that if that was " discontinued, what reason was there for a choir or prebenda- " ries—they had better all become parish priests only."* The answer contained an unconscious prophecy, or maybe Lord Harborough saw the change that was soon to come over the church. Towards the end of last century Abp. Drummond made a fruitless effort to avert the approaching doom by suggesting a somewhat radical reform of the college. He proposed that the number of canons should be reduced, residence enforced, and specific duties in the church assigned to them. The proposals were unfortunately blindly resisted by the chapter. Little did they think their institution had but seventy more years to live before sentence would be pronounced upon it. The Evangelical revival had already begun to arouse both clergy and people to a sense of their responsibilities, and this was followed by the Oxford movement. Early in the pre-

---

* Note-book of Sir R. Kaye.

sent century the cry for church reform was heard throughout the land. In 1835, on the recommendation of Sir Robert Peel, a royal commission was appointed to consider the general state of the Established Church. The "Church Commissioners," as they were called, turned their attention to the re-modelling of dioceses and the re-distribution of church property, and they issued four reports in quick succession. The legislature made no delay in making provision for carrying into effect the changes they recommended. The collegiate churches of Ripon and Manchester were raised to the dignity of episcopal sees; a thorough re-distribution of episcopal dioceses was made, and it was now that the county of Nottingham was subtracted from York and annexed to Lincoln, the change taking full effect in 1841; the revenues of episcopal sees were more equally divided and certain pluralities done away with; the number of archdeaconries was increased and all peculiar and exempt jurisdictions abolished: the peculiar of Southwell ceased to exist in 1846.

The reforms so far were made in the right direction, though they did not go far enough, more particularly in the matter of the increase of the number of episcopal sees. But the recommendations of the commissioners with regard to the cathedral and collegiate churches, which formed the next subject for legislation, was a signal failure: their work was hasty and ill-advised; it was far too radical in spirit; the commissioners would not pause to consider the objects for which these institutions had been founded originally, and how, by a correction of the abuses which had grown up in them, and by a re-distribution of capitular property, they might have been made to serve those objects, whereby, in fact, the end which the commissioners had in view might have been effectually attained; they preferred to make a clean sweep of them and to apply their property in their own method. When Parliament came to consider the subject, it was argued that the cathedral and collegiate churches no longer fulfilled the objects for which they were founded, that money must be found to meet the many spiritual wants of the country at large, and that the sinecures in these institutions would supply a fund ready to hand for the purpose. A bill called the *Ecclesiastical Duties and Revenues Bill* was introduced by Lord John Russell into the House of Commons in 1838. It proposed to suppress all canonries, excepting from four to six in each of our cathedral churches, and to place their estates in the hands of the Ecclesiastical Commissioners, who had been appointed in '36 a body corporate with perpetual succession to carry out such of the recommendations of the commissions of '35 as had, or should, become law by Act of Parliament. The opposition of the capitular bodies to the bill, and in fact of the whole church, was great, and stress of business caused it to be abandoned after the second reading. It was introduced again in the next session and received a like fate. On its third introduction, with slight alterations, in 1840, the government determined to push it through in the face of all opposition. Its opponents in the House of Commons reserved themselves for a grand effort when the bill should reach the committee stage. Mr. Pusey was chosen to move an amendment to the motion "that the Speaker leave the chair"; and Mr. Gladstone, in one of the greatest rhetorical displays of his early career, was ably supported by Sir T. Dyke-Acland, Mr. Acland, Sir R. Inglis, and others. After a long debate, however, the original motion was carried, and in due course the bill unfortunately became law.*

The opposition had left no stone unturned to avert what is now generally looked upon as almost a calamity, but in vain. The bill rested almost entirely on the responsibility of the Primate and the Bishop of London, who were both on the commission. The three other bishops on the commission were not prepared to press it. The remaining bishops on the bench were unanimously and actively opposed to it. During the sessions of '38, '39, and '40, up to June 2nd, no less than 228 petitions were presented against it, containing nearly 15,000 signatures, and including petitions from both universities and many of the cathedral and collegiate chapters. There was only one presented in its favour, with 22 signatures! These figures speak for themselves. The object for which the commission was appointed was "to consider the state of the "cathedral and collegiate churches with a view to render them "most conducive to the efficiency of the Established Church." "To render *them*," not *their money* only: the very principle of the bill was utterly unsound. It was an awkward attempt, says Mr. Freeman, at reform, made in utter ignorance of the history and nature of the institutions—instead of reforming them, it merely crippled them. The commissioners were to consider not the revenues only, but the "*duties* and revenues"

* 3 & 4 Vict., c. 113.

of capitular bodies. In dealing previously with the "episcopal duties and revenues" they had troubled themselves to consult the bishops severally with regard to both points before drawing up their report.* In this case, however, no information was sought or obtained as to the *duties* of capitular bodies, and when the several chapters came forward to supply the want, offering plans whereby the object in view might be attained without resource being had to radical changes in their constitution or wholesale suppression, the commissioners actually refused all communication with them with the words "*functi officio;* we have made our report."† The chapter of Exeter, with one or two others, made a second attempt while the bill was in progress, and the government paused to consider their schemes, but they were finally declined on the recommendation of the Primate and the Bishop of London. It is difficult to reconcile this action on the part of Bishop Blomfield with the words of the charge he had delivered to his clergy only a few years before; when he said that no comprehensive scheme of improvement could be made, nor could anything be done with any prospect of success or with safety to the church, except after careful inquiry into the circumstances of every diocese. Mr. Gladstone, giving his reasons for objecting to the bill, said that, while it involved a violation of the rights of property, it would be no remedy for the abuses that had crept into the cathedral system, and it would frustrate the great objects for which cathedrals had of old been established. And Mr. Freeman, thirty years later, bears testimony in part to the fulfilment of that view: our cathedral churches, he writes, have indeed vastly improved during those thirty years; but it has been almost wholly because they have shared in a general improvement, hardly at all by virtue of the changes which were specially meant to improve them. But note that he adds, it is quite impossible that our cathedral institutions can stay in the state in which they now are—a state which satisfies no party. Had Lord Melbourne's government paused in its work of spoliation, had the suggestions of Mr Pusey's amendment been adopted— that information should be collected, etc., as contemplated by the statutes of the several foundations, and that the visitors and bishops, after consultation, should draw up such plans as

* First Report of the Church Commissioners, 17 March, 1835.

† Second Report of the Church Commissioners, 4 March, 1836.

might in their judgment be best calculated to render them
most conducive to the efficiency of the church and to providing
for the cure of souls—then surely that end might have been
attained without practically destroying them. If the legislation had been directed to making a re-distribution of capitular
property, to fixing the duties of the members of our capitular
bodies, and to making adequate regulations for the performance of those duties,* then surely the existing parochial
destitution and the pressing spiritual wants of the people
would have been met, and our noble cathedrals would once
more have taken their proper position in the country, the
source from which the spiritual guidance of the people would
flow, and the head in which the affections of people and clergy
alike might centre.

It may be asked, what has all this got to do with Southwell, since it was not a cathedral church. But it is on the
eve of becoming a cathedral church, and the grand mistake
of the commissioners lay in their failing to see that the time
was at hand when it would be absolutely necessary to sub-
divide the dioceses of Lincoln and Lichfield and to form the
counties of Nottingham and Derby into a separate diocese.
Had it been merely a question, as they evidently in their
haste thought it was a question, of suppressing the college
and applying the funds in a more useful way, or of letting it
continue its humdrum existence, doing little or no good to
itself or to the church at large, then would they have been
clearly right in the recommendations they made. The criti-
cism which characterized the canonries of Southwell as sinecures was a very fair one. As we have seen, each prebendary
came into residence only once in four years, and for so light a
duty the remuneration was large, notwithstanding the fact
that owing to the system of letting their estates on the system
of fines, which had long prevailed, the greater part of the
real value of the church's property was enjoyed by the lay-
holders.† But this evil might have been remedied by placing

* See Mr. Gladstone's speech on Mr. Pusey's amendment.

† From the custom of letting their estates on the system of fines
the annual incomes of the owners of church property—who were
either corporate bodies, or, in the case of individuals, without power
to bequeath to their natural heirs—were gradually reduced far below
the real value of the property. I will endeavour to explain the system briefly. The property is leased in two ways, either for a period
of, say, 21 years or for such length of time as three persons, whose

names are inserted in the lease, shall happen to live. (In the property of the prebendaries and chapter of Southwell there were 43 leases for years, and 23 leases for lives.) At the end of 7 years, or when a life falls out of the lease, as the case may be, the lessee or purchaser may renew his lease for 7 fresh years (to be added on to his remaining 14), or put in a new life, by paying a *fine* of from 1¼ to 1½ years' income. (The chapter of Southwell accepted 1½ years' purchase.) Thus an estate worth £2,000, producing, therefore, at 5 per cent. interest, an annual income of £100, might be leased originally for its full value. At the end of 7 years the lease would be renewed by the payment of a fine of £150 or 1½ years' purchase. At the third renewal the value of the property to the owner or lessor would be reduced to £450, representing an income of about £22 instead of £100, and its value to the tenant would be increased by the corresponding amount. A similar reduction would result in the case of a lease for lives. By such a system the lessors were in a great measure dependent upon the fines paid for renewals, and in the case of leases for lives there was necessarily much uncertainty as to the time when the fines would fall in. The large capital of such corporate bodies as the Ecclesiastical Commissioners enables them to allow the leases to run out, and thus they can realise the actual value of the property. But the case of the prebendaries of Southwell was very different. Being very often men advanced in years, they were unwilling to forego the fines, which formed a material part of their income, by running their individual lives against the three lives inserted in a lease; nor could they afford to wait even so long as 21 years. By pursuing such a course they well knew that they would be only denying themselves in the interests of their successors in their prebends. On the contrary, there are stories of jobbery practised by them in these matters. It is said of a certain archbishop that, immediately after a near relation of his, to whom he had given a prebendal stall, had been lucky enough to receive the fines for three renewals in a short space of time, he transferred him to another stall which happened to fall vacant at the time, from which he had every prospect of reaping additional pecuniary benefits. One pities the unfortunate man who succeeded to the former stall with a lease which had probably had three young lives just put into it. We must add that in many leases there was also an annual rent reserved: thus, if an estate were worth £150 per annum, the fine would be set as if it were worth £100, and the tenant be bound to pay to the owner the sum of £50 annually. It is to be remembered, too, that the leases in many cases were of long standing, sometimes some centuries old; and while the actual value of the estate increased, the nominal value of the reserved rent would remain the same, the value of money at the same time decreasing.—See Short's *Church History*, pp. 89, 90.

It is convenient here to make a short extract from the Second Report of the Church Commissioners relative to Southwell: the chapter consists of sixteen prebendaries, who keep residence in rotation, each for three months, and are entitled to an allowance of £85 each towards the expenses of such residence: at the end of each rota, being a term of four years, a division of the fines received for renewals [of the leases of capitular property, I take it, as distinct from the whole of the property in the hands of the Ecclesiastical Commissioners, a course which has been pursued by many of our capitular bodies.

But it is no use crying over spilt milk. The suppression of the college of canons at Southwell is a historical fact; and it only remains for us to give a few details of the way in which it was carried out. The Ecclesiastical Duties and Revenues Bill, so far as related to Southwell, provided that all the canonries should be suspended, excepting one which was to be annexed to the archdeaconry of Nottingham;* and that

prebendal property] during that period, after deducting the customary payments and allowances, is made in equal portions among the prebendaries. There is a vicar general and commissary, whose net yearly revenue is £13 0s. 7d.; and six vicars choral, who are entitled on an average to £25 per annum each out of the chapter revenues. The prebendaries divide the surplus net revenue equally among themselves. Five of the vicars reside in houses assigned to them, and a sixth in a house which he occupies as vicar of Southwell. The gross yearly income is £2,211. Present average yearly payments, £1,119; and net income, subject to temporary changes, £954.

* The clause runs: "And be it enacted, that in the Collegiate "Church of *Southwell* the canonries now vacant, and all the other "canonries except the canonry now held by the Archdeacon of "Nottingham, as vacancies occur shall be suspended." In committee the Earl of Lincoln moved as an amendment: "That, in the "Collegiate Church of Southwell, the canonries, as vacancies occur, "except the canonry now held by the Archdeacon of Nottingham, "shall be suppressed until only four remain, and that such canons "shall be residentiaries."—His arguments were what may be called "sentimental," and he failed, equally with those who followed on the same side, to point to the necessity of preserving the chapter so that it might form the chapter of a new see.—Lord John Russell refused to accede; Mr. G. H. Vernon also opposed the amendment as inconsistent with the principle laid down by the commissioners; and Sir E. Sugden spoke against it.—Sir R. Inglis said that the taking away of stalls and other appendages of cathedral and collegiate churches was injuring the hold which the establishment had upon the people, and diminishing the inducements which the higher classes have to bring up their children to the church. The church is bound to supply spiritual instruction, but not from funds appropriated by law to totally different purposes.—Mr. Goulburn, while not opposing the bill, considered this part of it inconsistent with the amended report of the commissioners, which implied that all the paraphernalia of this collegiate church should be continued as before.—Colonel Robertson thought there was nothing to justify so stringent a clause. —Mr. Gladstone, having previously spoken at length against the whole bill, did not take part in the debate.—Division on the question "That these words be inserted:" ayes 14, noes 54, majority 40.

the benefices in the patronage of the prebendaries should be transferred so as to become vested, as the prebends fell in respectively, partly in the Bishop of Ripon and partly in the Bishop of Manchester.* In the following year an act was passed amending these provisions.† By this act the one remaining canonry was to be suspended, and it was provided that the vicarage of Southwell should be constituted a rectory, competently endowed out of the confiscated estates, and that on the next avoidance of the benefice the Archdeacon of Nottingham should become *ipso facto* rector, and that the rectory should thenceforth be permanently annexed to the archdeaconry.‡ It was left to the discretion of the Ecclesiastical Commissioners to carry out these provisions, and their recommendations were made law from time to time by order of the Queen in Council. As each canonry fell vacant, after the passing of the acts of '40 and '41, all the property and rights attached to it, except the right of patronage, became vested in the Ecclesiastical Commissioners. But before long the commissioners devised a more convenient method of dealing with the matter, and they drew up a scheme whereby the

---

* The chapter patronage remained with the chapter until it ceased to exist with the death of the last canon. † 4 & 5 Vict., c. 39.

‡ It so happened that the Archd. of Nottingham never became Rector of Southwell. Soon after the Act of '40 was passed the Vicarage of Southwell fell vacant, and the Venerable Archdeacon Wilkins, holding the patronage as Prebendary of Normanton, nominated his son, Mr J. Murray Wilkins, who was instituted on the 29th of December in that year. In the following spring the Act of Amendment described above was passed, and the Vicarage was finally constituted a Rectory by order in council gazetted November 9, '41, whereby also the Rector was empowered to employ an assistant-curate (not a minor canon) to be licensed by the Bishop of Lincoln, who, as holding the patronage of the Archdeaconry, became patron also of the Rectory. Dr. George Wilkins died in '65, and was succeeded in the Archdeaconry by Rev. Henry Mackenzie, incumbent of Tydd S. Mary. As, however, Mr. Murray Wilkins, Rector of Southwell, was still living, Archdeacon Mackenzie could not fulfil what seems to have been the intention of the Act of '41 by becoming Rector in virtue of his Archdeaconry. It was proposed to Mr. Murray Wilkins that he should exchange livings with the Archdeacon, but he declined to accede to that proposal. Under these circumstances it was thought advisable that so much of the Act of '41 as related to the Archdeacon of Nottingham should be repealed, and this was done by an Act of Amendment passed in the year '66 (29 & 30 Vict., c. 111). At the next avoidance, occasioned by the death of Mr. Murray Wilkins in 1880, the Bishop of Lincoln presented to the benefice the Rev. J. J Trebeck, who had for a short time previously discharged the cure of souls as curate in charge.

48

entire estates of the chapter and remaining prebendaries might be transferred to their hands, they granting to them an equivalent money payment agreed upon between themselves and the chapter. The *Gazette* of August 1st, 1848, contains the scheme, and the order in council by which it was ratified.

In the year '46 the canons then living were empowered to elect one of their number perpetual residentiary, but power was reserved to any remaining at his death to undertake residence again or to appoint a deputy. The Ven. George Wilkins, Archdeacon of Nottingham and Prebendary of Normanton, was appointed to fill the post. He died in '65. Mr. Thomas Henry Shepherd, Prebendary of Beckingham, was now the sole surviving member of the chapter, but he was unable through age to undertake residence, and appointed Mr. Murray Wilkins to be his deputy residentiary. On February 11th, 1873, Mr. Shepherd died, and with his death the chapter ceased to exist.

There is still, however, one link left with the time-honoured institution of the past. On the recommendation of the commissioners the number of vicars choral was reduced from six to two, and their style was changed from "vicar choral" to "minor canon." The two minor canons, then, continued to be elected by the chapter as long as it lived, as the vicars choral had been elected of old. The office was held, at the time of Mr. Shepherd's death, by the Revs. Alfred Tatham and R. F. Smith, who succeeded Mr. J. F. Dimock on his promotion to Barnburgh Rectory in '63. Mr. Tatham died in 1878, and Mr. Smith still lives to connect the past with the present, and, we hope, with the future. It is a curious, if somewhat melancholy fact, that when Mr. Smith duly notified the death of Mr. Tatham in the chapter records, there remained only a few lines on the very last page of the last volume to be filled up. Upon whom will the duty devolve of paying the like tribute to the memory of the last vicar choral of the college of Southwell?

The history of the collegiate church has at length drawn to a close. One word about the cathedral church of the future. At last Southwell is on the eve of becoming a bishopric. Regret has already been expressed that the commissioners did not see fit to recommend this change instead of the suppression of the college—a regret that is felt all the more when we remember that the chance of restoring the canonries was not lost till as late as the year '73. Only five years later was the act* passed by which the counties of Nottingham and Derby

* Bishoprics Act, 41 & 42 Vict., c. 68.

are to be formed into a separate diocese. The carrying out of the act has been delayed by the tardiness with which the subscriptions to the bishopric fund have come in; but the meeting at the Mansion House on the 1st of June last has given an impetus to subscribers; some £15,000 has been collected since that date, and, as I write, less than £13,000 are wanted to make up the necessary sum. The ultimate endowment of the bishopric will be £3,500 a year, together with an episcopal residence; towards this income the see of Lincoln will contribute £500 a year, and the see of Lichfield £300. The Ecclesiastical Commissioners have power to create new archdeaconries in the diocese, and to transfer any archidiaconal dignity from Lincoln and Lichfield to the new cathedral church; also to transfer the patronage of any benefices situate in the diocese from the other sees to the new see; and to found honorary canonries, and to transfer to Southwell such honorary canons of Lincoln and Lichfield as hold benefices in the new diocese and themselves consent to the transfer.

It must not be thought, however, that immediately on the formation of the bishopric the whole machinery of diocesan work will be set going. The motive power will be there in the person of the bishop, but the greater part of the machinery will have to be made. And the making of this machinery will be a slow and gradual process, stretching over many years. There will be all the Diocesan Societies to come into being: a Church Building Society, for instance, to promote the building, restoration, and endowment of churches; an Additional Curates' Society, and a Curates' Augmentation Fund; a Diocesan Board of Education, to provide for the inspection of church schools for the poor, and the examination of their pupil teachers and scholars in religious knowledge— the board, or a separate society, would find work to do in the way of building or enlarging schools, besides distributing information and giving advice on educational topics, and seeking means to avert the unnecessary transfer of church schools to school boards. These and like societies are all necessary for the efficient organization of a diocese nowadays. But it must be borne in mind that they are supported entirely by voluntary contributions. They have to be worked, therefore, by means of large committees consisting of the chief clergymen and influential laymen of the diocese. Later on, we may hope, resident canonries will be formed. To each one

D

will be attached some definite duties: to one, perhaps, the inspectorship of schools and the secretaryship of the Diocesan School Board; to another the secretaryship of several other Diocesan Societies, which would fully occupy the time of one who has heart and soul in his work, as those who have occupied like positions, too often in addition to a cure of souls, can testify. For a satisfactory and efficient fulfilment of such duties the personal and perpetual residence of the canons holding them in the cathedral city would be absolutely necessary, so as to permit frequent intercourse with the bishop. The holding of an annual Diocesan Conference, now found to be so advantageous for the general welfare of the dioceses in which they have been established of late years, would naturally be a part of the growing organization. And lastly, with regard to the chapter. The capitular body is essentially the council of the bishop. Composed of the archdeacons and the honorary canons—the picked men of the diocese—it will serve to connect the various parts of the diocese with its true centre, the cathedral church, and will work with the bishop and assist him with its counsel and advice in all matters concerning the general well-being of his diocese.

The object of these pages has been to endeavour to connect the past, present, and future of our church into a continuous history. In its earliest days, as a missionary centre, it successfully performed its task of converting the people, and of firmly establishing the Christian church in their midst by means of the priests it sent forth. The college of secular canons at Southwell has lived its life and died—died like many of our historic institutions in these days of radical and too often ignorant reform have died. And now, once again, under changed circumstances and conditions, Southwell is about to resume its labours and carry on the work which its priests long ago begun. Once again, after centuries almost of spiritual apathy and consequent misfortune, the church is to raise its head among its fellows like the mother church of old. And much is to be learnt from its past history, whereby a repetition of its short-comings and long-standing abuses may be avoided, and its future history be made to form a happier and brighter page in its annals.

CHAPTER II.

HISTORY OF THE FABRIC: DATES.

The historical ground-plan of the existing church explains itself, but this little work would not be complete if we failed to give the authorities for the dates to be assigned to the various parts of the fabric. This part of our subject has been so thoroughly worked out by Mr. Dimock,[*] late a vicar-choral, that we have to give but little more than the gist of his arguments. No part of the present fabric, with the exception of one or two fragments, dates farther back than the 12th century. But we have abundant evidence that a considerable stone church existed at any rate in the previous century. Thomas Stubbs,[†] the biographer of the Archbishops of York, tells us that Abp. Kinsius (1050-1060) added a lofty stone tower to Beverley church and put two large bells in it, and that he gave bells of like magnitude to Stow and Southwell. Stow, we know, was rebuilt in 1057.[‡] To receive the bells a campanile must have been recently built at Southwell. Perhaps the church had been entirely rebuilt. At any rate it is a significant fact that Aldred, the successor of Kinsius, out of certain lands purchased at his own cost formed prebends at Southwell, and built refectories wherein the canons might take their common meals. The Norman parts of the church, as it stands, contain unmistakeable evidences of an earlier building. In the north transept, over the doorway leading to the newel by which one ascends the central tower there is a large sculptured stone which is worked into the building in such a way as to shew at a glance that it is old material used up again. It is supposed by competent judges to have formed the tympanum of an *early* Norman doorway. Again, Mr. Petit, in a paper read at a meeting of the Archæo-

---

[*] In a contribution to the Journal of the Brit. Arch. Ass., Jan. No., 1853.   [†] *Twysden's* X *Scriptores.*

[‡] *Florence of Worcester* and *Henry of Huntingdon.*

logical Institute held at Lincoln in 1848, remarked that
"a few years ago some foundations consisting of rubble work,
" and exceeding at least two feet in thickness, running north
"and south, were discovered within the area of the north
" transept, the western face being about eight feet from that
"of the eastern wall of the transept." Old Mr. Gregory,
who was superintending the repairs of the building at that
time and still remains at his post, does not now remember the
fact here recorded, though he can call to mind the visits of
Mr. Petit. It is to be hoped that the clue will be followed
out when the flooring of the transepts is taken up for repairs,
which is to be done very soon. And lastly there is the evidence of some valuable fragments which were found, during
repairs some thirty years ago, in the foundations of the south
wall of the nave. These have unfortunately mysteriously
disappeared,* but Mr. Dimock has put on record a careful
description of them with illustrations, one or two of which
are sketched in an accompanying plate (No. III). The mouldings were apparently of the character of Norman work, some
of them unlike anything to be found in the present building,
while the sections of others are quite different from the sections
of similar mouldings used in the existing Norman structure.
The conclusion then we come to about this early church is
that it was considerably enlarged and ornamented, possibly
altogether rebuilt, about the middle of the 11th century.

1110. . is the date assigned to the Nave and Transepts, the
Norman portions of the fabric. Plan II. shews the 12th
century church complete, to which we shall devote a short
chapter later on. In the *Registrum Album* is preserved an
undated letter which makes a direct reference to the building
of the church of S. Mary of Suwell, and in assigning a date
to the letter the date of the building itself is fixed. It was
written by an Abp. Thomas, addressed to all his parishioners
in Nottinghamshire, asking for their alms to assist in defraying
the cost of the building. Now there were three archbishops
named Thomas—Thomas I., 1070-1100; Thomas II., 1109-
1114; and Thomas de Corbridge, 1299-1303. The last-named
is out of the question, because the bull of Alexander III. in

---

* A dozen or more such fragments, arch-mouldings, capitals, &c.,
of untold interest both historically and architecturally, were placed
for safe keeping *(sic)* in the cloister, not one of which now remains
to tell its tale. How or when they were removed no one at present
seems to know.

1171 mentions as an *ancient* custom the Pentecostal synod which the archbishop in this very letter says he is instituting. Thomas I. is not likely to have undertaken so great a work, since his episcopate was occupied in restoring the fallen fortunes of the canons of York. The two sons of Sweyn, with their Northmen, had put the Norman garrison to the sword and surrendered the noble minster to the flames. The conqueror, in savage vengeance, had completed the work of devastation in city and county. Thomas I. found it necessary to set about rebuilding the whole church: he completed the nave and transepts, but it is probable that he contented himself with merely restoring the old Saxon chancel. With such a gigantic work in hand he would scarcely have turned his attention to Southwell, whose church stood intact; moreover his name is nowhere mentioned in connection with Southwell. Thomas II., on the contrary, finding the church at York completed, turned his attention to the outlying parts of his diocese, and raised Southwell, as we have seen, to the position of a mother church. Nothing is more natural than that he should have ordained that an annual synod should be held there, and have replaced the earlier structure by one larger and more suited to its higher dignity. The architectural details, too, of the building conform to the later date. To take a single instance, look at the compact masonry of Southwell nave and compare it with that of any known 11th century Norman work, with the loose-jointed masonry of the west front of Lincoln for instance, and the point is at once settled.

The Early English Choir, . . 1230 . . 1250.—There can be little doubt that the choir was begun and finished in the episcopate of Walter Gray, and that the dates given are approximately correct. I. In Torre's *Collectanea*, in the library at York, is preserved an *Indulgence*, addressed by Walter Gray to the bishops and archdeacons of his province, granting a release of thirty days from penance enjoined to all who being truly penitent should contribute to the construction of the church of Southwell *(ad constructionem dictæ fabricæ)*, since the means of the church were insufficient for the consummation of the fabric a while since begun *(ad inceptæ dudum fabricæ consummationem)*. Torre gives 1235 as the date of the indulgence, but the document itself says "in the 19th year of our pontificate," which according to Drake would be 1233. But the difference is of no account. II. The *Registrum Album*

contains the foundation deeds of two chantries at the altar of
S. Thomas by Robert de Lexinton, canon of Southwell. By
the same authority we know that the later of the two chantries was founded in 1241. In the foundation deed of the
earlier chantry are the words, *In capella beati Thomæ Martyris
in novo opere,* "in the chapel of S. Thomas the Martyr *in the
new work.*" The situation of this chapel is not known. The
conclusion is that by about 1241 the building of the choir
was so far advanced to allow of divine service being performed
in it. Chantries were often founded and services held in
churches before their building was completed. III. The
Registrum Album contains many deeds of donations to the
fabric. There are about thirty of them in all. Most of them
bear no dates, which are seldom found affixed to deeds earlier
than the 14th century; but Mr. Dimock has shewn that they
are all to be referred to the reign of Henry III., with the
exception of two 15th century ones. IV. The capitular acts
af 1248 contain two significant provisions: that the *custos* of
the fabric should render a yearly account of all his receipts;
and that the several canons should pay to the fabric fund a
fifteenth of their prebends for three years to come. I am
inclined to think that by the year 1248 the choir had been
nearly if not quite finished, and that these provisions were
enacted in view of such additional buildings as were in con-
templation, the date of which we are about to consider.

The North Transept Chapel, *c.* 1260.—The architectural
details of this building give the chief clue to its date. It is
clear that it is a distinct work from the choir, and it is equally
clear that it must have been undertaken within a few years
after the choir was finished, and that it was left in an unfinished state. The *Registrum Album* records certain acts
passed in chapter in 1260, which clearly refer to some work
recently undertaken and then in progress. No doubt this
chapel is the work referred to. They provide that the accounts
of the custos of the fabric, shewing his *receipts and expenses,*
be duly examined. It was decreed also that "the custos
"shall not begin any new work, in the church or outside,
"without the consent of his brother canons in general convo-
"cation." These passages seem to imply that the custos had
commenced some work which did not meet with general
approval on account of a want of means to meet the expense
incurred thereby. This would account for the building being
left in a somewhat unfinished state.

The Cloister,..1270..1285.—The cloister is decidedly
somewhat later than the north transept chapel, to the east wall
of which it is attached, and quite a distinct work. Its architecture shews it to be slightly earlier than the chapter-house,
but its close connection with the vestibule thereto inclines
one to assign a late date to it: c. 1285 rather than c. 1270.
But the point cannot be satisfactorily determined.

The Chapter-house and its Vestibule,..1285..1300..—
Abp. John Romanus, in the statutes which he granted to the
college in 1294, orders that the prebendal houses of the foreign
canons, which had fallen into ruin, be properly repaired
within a year; and he further orders that in case of neglect
heavy fines be enforced, the fines to be devoted to, the fabric
of the *new* chapter-house *(ad fabricam novi capituli)*. This
expression would bear three constructions: that by 1294 the
chapter-house had been completed, that it was then in course
of construction, or that preparations were being made for its
commencement. The fact that in the original glazing of the
windows the arms of the Queen of Edward I., the yellow
castles of Castile, appeared, favours an early date, since
Eleanor of Castile died in 1290. On the other hand, the issue
of an indulgence of forty days pardon by Boniface [VIII.,
1294-1303] seems to point to a later date. The very close
similarity in plan of the chapter-houses of York and Southwell has an important bearing upon their dates. Southwell
is a copy of York on a small scale, but equal to it, or even
surpassing it, in beauty. I am inclined to think they were
designed by the same hand, under the superintendence of
Abp. John Romanus, and very probably they were simulta-
neously in course of construction.* Abp. John was the son
of the treasurer John Romanus, whose name is known in
connection with the transepts of York. He became archbishop in 1286, laid the foundation stone of the beautiful
nave of York in 1291, and died, long before his work was
carried out, in 1296.

Some of the above dates receive confirmation from the
numerous indulgences which were granted during the 13th
century. Torre's *Collectanea* contains the abstract of a "letter
"of request issued out from the chapter of York for to
"collect the alms and charitable contributions of the people
"within the city, diocese, and province of York, for the

* See remarks in note at close of next chapter.

" support of the fabric of the church of S. Mary of Suthwell."
Its date is 1352.   The letter recited the indulgences formerly
granted to those who should "charitably relieve the church,
" viz. from Pope Boniface, forty days of pardon; from the
" Popes Urban, Celestine, Gregory, Honorius, Innocent, Cle-
" ment, and Alexander, one year and forty days of pardon
" from each; likewise all the indulgences granted and con-
" firmed by archbishops and bishops, especially of Walter,
" Sewald, Godfrey, William, Archbishops of York and Bishops
" of Dunhelm, forty days from each."   Omitting Boniface,
these are exactly the names, singularly enough, of the popes
who lived during the reign of Henry III., excepting that
only one Gregory is mentioned instead of two.   The names
of the archbishops doubtless refer to Walter de Gray (1216-
1256), Sewall de Bovill (1256-1258), and Godfrey de Ludham
(1258-1264).

The   Organ-screen, . . 1335 . . 1340 . . —In   the   *Registrum
Album* is preserved a license granted by Edward III. in 1337
for the free carriage of stone from the Mansfield quarry through
the forest of Sherwood.   It was granted in consequence of a
complaint made to the king by the canons that the king's
foresters had been and were in the habit of exacting toll for
the passage of the carts sent by them to fetch stone from their
quarry for the fabric of the church, contrary to the provisions
of the forest charta.   Evidently some considerable work was
in progress and the date of the organ-screen, as fixed by its
architecture, tallies well with the date of the license.

No exact date can be assigned to the Sedilia, which is of
the pure Decorated style; the inserted windows in the north
transept chapel late Decorated, and the inserted Perpendicular
windows of the nave.   These are given here in their chronological order, and are all 14th century work, except perhaps
the nave windows, which may be early 15th century.
The large west window certainly belongs to the 15th century.
The sedilia may perhaps be part of the work implied in the
"letter of request" quoted above, which would place their
date at 1355.   But the contributions which it was the object
of this letter to raise must have been devoted chiefly to the
many necessary repairs of the fabric about this time, as the
words " for the *support* of the fabric" imply.

CHAPTER III.

THE NORMAN CHURCH RESTORED.

The *Architect* of June 23rd, 1877, contains a remarkably pretty and effective drawing, by Mr. C. Hodgson Fowler, of Southwell Minster restored : represented, that is, as it would probably appear to us if the various parts of the present building had been allowed to retain their original form, with their high-pitched roofs, pyramidal spires, and original windows. It is accompanied by a ground-plan of the original Norman church complete. This, however, is less happy, for it is incorrect in more than one important point. Some thirty years ago the flooring of the choir was taken up, and Mr. Dimock was able to determine the length of the old Norman choir, and to satisfy himself on two other points, first that its east end was not apsidal, as it usually is in Norman churches, but square in form ; and secondly that it had aisles extending about half its length. About ten years ago the flooring of the aisles was again removed, this time for the special purpose of investigating the form of the termination of the Norman aisles. They were then found to terminate in circular apses, and accurate plans of the foundations were made.* Quite recently, under the direction of Mr. Christian, the foundations under the north transept chapel have been partially discovered in restoration. They are just sufficiently exposed to enable one to trace out the form and dimensions of the circular chapel, which, like its early English successor, opened out into the transept on its east side. It is from these data the plan (No. II.) of the original Norman church which appears in our plate has been worked out.

Beginning from the east end and working westwards I cannot do better than quote Mr. Dimock's observations which he made in a personal examination of the foundations—so far,

---

* The courtesy of Mr. R. D. Noble enabled me to make a rough copy of these plans.

that is, as they have been verified by the later excavations.
They were recorded by him in his account of the *Architectural
History of Southwell Church* published in the Journal of the
British Archæological Association for January, 1853. A
reference to the ground-plan will make them plain. "For
"some few feet at the east end, and from *p* to *r*, there
"remains a basement moulding—a small slope exactly like
"that round the outside of the nave and transepts—with
"one course of ashlar upon it through most of its length:
"beneath the bases of the two Early English pillars are also
"two or three stones of the second course of ashlar, the bot-
"toms of these bases being about 20 in. above the level of
"this Norman basement moulding. At the corner *p* is a
"rectangular nook of about 9 in. in depth, exactly the same
"as is formed at the external corners of the transepts and of
"the western towers by the projections of the Norman but-
"tresses. There can be no doubt, therefore, but that this
"was an external basement; and that, as in the present choir
"so in the Noman one, the aisles did not extend the whole
"length. Between *p* and *q*, therefore, was a buttress, and
"this is much of the same width as the buttresses in corres-
"ponding places of the nave and transepts. But at *q*, instead
"of a projection of only 9 in. from the line of the wall, there
"is a projection of nearly 18 in.; just the projection of the
"western towers, independently of their buttresses, from the
"aisle walls. Hence I conclude that the east end was flanked
"by corner turrets, an arrangement that has also a parallel in
"the far-projecting corner buttresses, with their surmounting
"pinnacles, at the east end of the present choir; had there
"not been such an arrangement, no greater thickness of wall
"would have been required, and this corner of the south
"transept would have presented the same ground-plan as the
"corner of the south transept shewn in the plate. Enough
"of the basement is to be seen extending northwards from *p*
"to shew that the east end of the choir was square." This
much was Mr. Dimock enabled to determine with certainty.
At *r*, and for three or four feet onwards, he discovered rubble
foundation extending some few feet southwards, which he
rightly thought to indicate the termination of the Norman
aisle, without, however, being able to ascertain its circular
shape. Passing over this he followed what appeared to be the
plinth or basement moulding again for some little distance.
He was prevented from pushing his investigation any further

by the woodwork of the stalls and galleries which in those days occupied the aisle and the spaces between the piers.

In the later excavations the foundations of what proved to be semi-circular apses were more fully examined. In the north aisle, which had not before been opened up, they were thoroughly discovered; in the south aisle the examination was only partial, but enough was done to shew their form to be the same. Our plate (Plan III.) shews the ground-plan and elevation of the foundations in the north aisle. It appears that the ashlar walling of the apse, of which a considerable amount remains, was carried to a great depth—5 ft. below the top of the plinth. In the south aisle, however, there were only 2½ ft. We conclude, therefore, that the flooring of the apses was considerably lower than the level of the aisles. By this means the chapels would naturally gain in height. The diameter of the apse was 8½ ft. in the north aisle, and 9 ft. in the south. The breadth of the aisles themselves was somewhat more than a foot less than that of the present aisles, the Norman walls being by a corresponding amount thicker than the Early English walls.

So much for the aisles. In considering the general arrangement of the Norman choir we have to go to the eastern piers of the lantern-tower and study the abutment of the new work upon the old. Here we have the engaged semi-cylindrical columns, which formed the responds of the choir arches, still left, and above their capitals some of the old masonry attached to the tower-piers remains, as may be seen from the organ-loft. This masonry preserves to us the spring of the Norman arch, shewing billet-mould, and above that the hatched string-course that ran along under the triforium. The capitals of the columns are some 2 ft. higher than the level of the capitals of the nave arches, while the string-course under the triforium is on exactly the same level as that in the nave. The floor of the body of the choir was probably, therefore, about 2 ft. higher than that of the nave and side aisles. In this case the plinth marked *e* in our plan (No. III.) is easily explained as being the basement, as Mr. Dimock surmised, of a wall bounding the raised flooring, and carrying, perhaps, a wooden screen dividing the choir from its aisles. In the nave aisles a similar basement moulding is carried from the west wall of the transepts round the responds of the first nave arches. The external height of the choir and the arrangement of its triforium and clerestory must have been precisely like the corresponding features of the nave. This is proved by the level of the string-courses under the triforium stages being the same; by the exact correspondence of the arches opening from the transepts into the nave and choir aisles, and of the arches above them opening into the triforium; and, on the exterior, by the weather-moulding of the old Norman roof, which may be seen on the eastern side of the lantern-tower, as well as by a remnant of the corbel-table with nebule moulding which supported the eave-roof.

Now we come to the pier arcades. The length of the aisle was about 29 ft. This would admit of an arcading of two arches only, and these of less span than those in the nave, which are about 13 ft. Allowing 12 ft. for the column and two responds, we have 17 ft. left for the two arches. This gives 8½ ft. for the span of each arch, which is exactly the amount computed by Mr. Dimock from the two or three feet of the springing of the first arch which, as we have seen, is left imbedded in the Early English structure. The fact that the height from the capital to the string-course is some 2 ft. less than in the nave proves of itself that the span of the choir arches was less than that of the nave arches. The measurements adopted in our plan must be very nearly correct.

Opening out into each transept on its eastern side there was originally an apsidal chapel, semi-circular in form, like those terminating the choir aisles, but somewhat larger. The large arches of communication still remain. In the south transept the span of the arch is 15 ft. It was walled up when in Early English times the apse was pulled down, and in the walling is inserted a blocked Norman window. Whence this window came I cannot say. It is similar in detail to the original windows of the nave, and, but for the fact that it is smaller than they, we might imagine that it came from the destroyed choir. Mr. Dimock thought it must have been a window of the adjoining chapel, and concluded, from its arch-moulding and from the straight string-course that is continued from the abacus, that the chapel was either rectangular or polygonal. Going to the outside we see imbedded in the masonry the inferior order of the arch. On each side of the arch a flat buttress runs up the wall to a point just under the end of the gable-moulding. Upon these the circular wall abutted, but it is singular that the ashlaring shews little sign of any building having been removed. The southern buttress contains

some old Norman material worked up : I refer to the short
string of zigzag running partly across it and continued in the
walling up of the arch. The string is broken by a Norman
shaft running up in the angle formed by the buttress, or
rather a projection from it, and the walling of the arch. Mr.
Petit has pointed out that the projection and the shaft lean
towards each other, as if it were intended that the former
should counteract the pressure of the arch. The capital of
the shaft is complete, and is possibly a part of the original
impost. The height of the gable-moulding indicates an upper
story to the apse, but no means of access to it now appears.
The horizontal moulding just above the crown of the arch
was probably connected with the flooring of this apartment.
In the north transept one of the jambs of the arch of communication has been cut back to give room for the pair of pointed
arches of the entrance into the Early English chapel which
has taken the place of the Norman one. The chapel is now
being restored, and one can just trace in the rubble of the
flooring the lines of the circular apse. Its diameter is about
12 ft. and the thickness of the wall about 4 ft., the same as
the walls of the nave, and a foot less than those of the transepts. The floor of the apse, like that of its successor and
like the similar apses of the choir aisles, was some 2 or 3 ft.
lower than the general level of the Norman church, as is
proved by the depth to which the ashlar-work of the remaining jamb is carried.

The building had a second story, and a small round-headed
doorway, now blocked up, gave access to the upper apartment
from the passage running round the middle stage of the transept. But this was a long and difficult way of reaching it,
and I am fully inclined to think that the space between the
apse and the wall of the choir aisle was occupied by a spiral
staircase. There is certainly no sign of such a staircase in
the foundation as at present exposed, but the space is now
occupied by the wall of the Early English chapel and a passage
that was made to run beside it. But signs of such an arrangement are not wanting. The staircase which now leads to the
upper apartment of the Early English building, just at the
top, turns round a shaft which stands in the very position
which the newel of the Norman staircase would have occupied.
Moreover this shaft is evidently part of an original newel, and
to it are attached a part of its old steps ; and, again, upon it
is placed a part of another shaft without doubt Norman, and

shewing Norman sculpture. Then there is the doorway between the chapel and the entrance to the choir aisle to be considered. It is a strange mixture of Norman, Early English (restored), and debased Perpendicular work. The last of these is little more than sixty years old. Without doubt the doorway is an instance of Early English patchwork. The Norman work must have come from the jambs of one of the windows of the destroyed choir. Then the question presents itself, why did the Early English builders pierce a Norman wall of 5 ft. 3 in. in thickness to make a doorway here? It could not have been meant for a side entrance to the chapel: such an additional entrance from the transept would have been quite unnecessary and decidedly inconvenient, as one would have had to make a sudden drop of 3 ft., as far as I can remember, to gain the side doorway of the chapel, which seems rather to have been connected with the choir aisle by the passage already mentioned. An easy answer is that they found a doorway already here, and widened it, intending to make a staircase to replace the newel they had destroyed because it interfered with the wall of their new chapel. This they immediately found impracticable, and changed their plan in favour of the present staircase from the choir aisle. The doorway they found would be the entrance to the old newel staircase, similar in shape and dimensions to those in other parts of the building. Its square head would account for the very depressed form of the present doorway. There is a third argument in favour of the newel, to be deduced from the plans of other Norman churches. Professor Willis, in his researches among the foundations of York Cathedral, was led to believe that in the Norman church, whose plan bore a close resemblance to that of Southwell, there was a similar arrangement. He says that the remains of this Norman staircase "may still be seen in the triforium of the choir at its western "extremity, but the rest of the staircase and turret have long "been destroyed." And he adds: "a spiral staircase, in the "same position, occurs at Norwich, and its use is to conduct "to the upper galleries of the church, and also to the upper "chapels of the apses; for these apses had commonly a chapel "on the triforium level as well as below."

This closes the consideration of the Norman church of the 12th century. Any changes which have been made in those parts of it which are now standing will be fully noticed in the following chapter.

NOTE.—It may be well to take this opportunity of adding a short note upon the mutual influence of York and Southwell with regard to their plan and structure. Professor Willis, in his *Architectural History of York*, has shewn that Abp. Thomas I., after the destruction of the Saxon church, commenced the entire re-building of it on a larger scale. The Norman foundations shew that he completed the nave and transepts, while there are no remains of any corresponding choir. The foundations of the Saxon chancel, however, with no side aisles, and apparently closely connected with the east walls of the transepts, remain, which led Professor Willis to believe that Thomas contented himself with a restoration of the small Saxon chancel. These foundations seem to indicate that the chancel, like the Saxon one at Ripon, had a square east end,* which would account for the peculiarity of the same peculiar feature in the Norman church of Southwell, built by Abp. Thomas II. some thirty years after his namesake's restoration of York. The same feature occurs again in the larger choir of York added by Abp. Roger some forty years later still, and Mr. Dimock asks, was it not the general plan in the diocese of York? The Norman nave and transepts, with their circular apses, of Southwell, are an evident repetition of the plan of Thomas I.'s church at York. Again, a glance at the plan of Abp. Roger's choir at York, with its secondary transepts, at once suggests a reason for the very similar plan adopted by Abp. Gray a hundred years later for his choir at Southwell.†

Here I have to add to my recent remarks on the chapter-houses of York and Southwell. Mr. Browne and Professor Willis are at strange variance in the dates they give for the commencement of York chapter-house. The former gives 1280, which the latter thinks to be too early by nearly fifty years. If Professor Willis's view on this point be correct, there can be no doubt that the plan of the grander chapter-house of York is a direct copy of Southwell. The beautiful combination of clerestory and triforium into one stage in the choir of Southwell may certainly be looked upon as the origin of the like arrangement in the later nave of York.

---

* Professor Willis, in his plan of this first church at York, puts a circular apse at the east end. He does not explain why, and I am at a loss to understand, except that this was the plan commonly adopted by the Norman builders.

† In connection with this subject see the series of comparative plans of York Minster, published by Professor Willis in the York volume of the Journal of the Arch. Inst.

CHAPTER IV.

THE FABRIC: ARCHITECTURAL DESCRIPTION.

In examining the minster in detail I propose to deal first with the exterior and then with the interior. The several parts of the interior I shall take in their chronological order; but I reserve the effigies, glazing, sepulchral slabs, and the like, for consideration in a separate chapter, so that the continuity of the description of the actual fabric may not be broken. With regard to the exterior, beginning with the west front, it will be well to go round to the east by the south side and return to the west entrance by the north, for by this means we shall be enabled again to make the acquaintance of the different parts in their historical order, from Norman to Early English, and thence to Decorated work. But the visitor must not fail to take some opportunity of going to the extreme north-west corner of the churchyard, whence one of the finest general views of the church may be seen.

South-West View.

Standing some distance from the south-west corner of the building we command at once the west front, the nave, the south transept, and the lantern tower; in fact a general view of the Norman building. Imagine a gable containing, perhaps, a circular window, with a row of arcading below it, all in the place of the large Perpendicular window filling the space between the western towers; take away the parapet walls of the aisle and clerestory, and imagine eave-roofs resting

on the nebule corbel-tables; and, lastly, remove the Norman
pinnacles from the lantern tower, and, placing them so as to
flank the gable of the transept, imagine the tower to be
crowned with a low pyramidal-shaped roof or spire, like the
one at Penmon Priory Church in Anglesea—imagine these
changes and you will form a very fair notion of what the
original Norman church was like. It is in terms of no mean
praise that Mr. Freeman says that "the grouping of the three
"towers is as perfect as it may well be."* In fact this is one
of the few great early churches in England which retain their
three great towers, and "this gives it a dignity hardly to be

* It is due to Mr. Freeman to say that these words were written
by him before the present spires were placed on the western towers.
The towers were then crowned by parapets and corner pinnacles in
imitation of the patched-up Norman work still seen on the lantern
tower. Many persons think that the architect has been ill-advised in
this part of the restoration, since he is unable to replace the corresponding low spire on the lantern tower. They seem to destroy the
"perfection of the grouping of the three towers," though they are
archæologically correct. But there can be no two opinions about the
advisability of Mr. Christian's restoration of the high-pitched roof
of the nave. In the interior the gain in effect has been so great as
to quite outweigh the objection advanced by some that the lantern
tower has been dwarfed thereby. The history of the western spires
may be briefly told. They appear in the sketch taken by W. Hollar
in 1672, and published in the following year in the first edition of
Dugdale's *Monasticon*, and shortly afterwards again in Thoroton's
Nottinghamshire. They were consumed by a disastrous fire which
happened in 1711, doing damage to the amount of £4,000. They
were restored immediately afterwards, and appear in the plates of
Mr. Dickenson's *Southwell*, 1787. Mr. James Essex, F.S.A., writes
(Add. MSS., 6768, c. 1780) "on each [tower] is a very heavey spire
covered with lead." They lastly were removed in 1801-2, in consequence of a rift appearing in the lower part of the north-west tower,
it being thought therefore that their great weight endangered the
safety of the structure. On this point we are assured, by the writer
of an article which appeared in *The Builder* of September 18th, 1880,
that "any fear is absurd: the towers would carry twice their weight."
One word as to the form of the present spires: the older drawings
represent them as coming down over the corbel-tables without any
slight cant outwards, and the latter form has been given to them on
the authority of a sketch by Turner, and this being minutely accurate
in other details, the architect, in whose possession the drawing now
is, could only think that the artist was equally accurate in this point.

" attained by much larger and more dignified churches, such
" as Worcester and Gloucester."* It may be compared, and
favourably so, with Rochester, which most nearly approaches
it in date and plan. The broad pilaster-like buttresses, dying
away into the nebule corbel-table which runs along the tops
of the walls, are a characteristic feature of Norman work : of
shallow projection, they can give little material support to
walls of four and five feet in thickness—they were used chiefly
to give relief to the flatness of the walls. One is struck by
the prevalence of the horizontal lines formed by the string-
courses which run round the towers, dividing them into stages.
In the lower stages they are continued along the nave and
transepts, embracing the buttresses, and in the original church
they encircled the whole building. They certainly detract
from the appearance of height, but on the other hand they
irresistibly carry the eye along the building, assisting the
mind to grasp it as a whole in a way that would be impossible
without them.†

The West Front.

The harmony of the Norman front has unfortunately been
entirely destroyed by the insertion of the large 15th century
window with the battlemented parapet above it, which occupies the space between the towers.‡ The towers themselves

---

* *Saturday Review*, August 5th, 1879.

† The writer of the article in *The Builder* applies the term *Roman-
esque* to the Norman building, and points out that many features of
the exterior are suggestive of the early churches of the Rhineland,
more especially the straight lines of the towers, the flat buttresses,
and the circular windows of the clerestory.

‡ In considering what was the original arrangement of the west
front we may note that " the triforium and clerestory passages were
" continued between the towers along the inside of this front. We
" may conjecture, therefore, that above the lower stage containing
" the west door there would be two tiers of arcading pierced occa-
" sionally for windows, which in the clerestory stage would perhaps

are a good example of Norman towers: it will be noticed that
the lower stages were originally left blank—for the round-
headed windows are quite modern insertions and not a restoration*—and the richness of the ornament gradually increases
as the eye travels upwards, until it rests upon the upper
stages adorned with rich arcading running right round them,
a device which, by carrying the eye upwards, counteracts the
effect of the horizontal lines. The arcading of the last stage
but one in the north-west tower, a series of intersecting
arches, is a common feature of advanced Norman work.
Were that part of the head of each round arch, which lies
between its points of intersection with the arch of either side
of it, omitted, there would remain an arcade of narrow pointed
arches‡; and this is exactly what does occur in the corresponding stage of the south tower. It was a favourite theory of
architects in the earlier part of the century that it was this

---

"be circular, corresponding with the other clerestory windows,"
(Mr. Dimock's *Arch.Hist.*), and the whole would probably be crowned
with a gable. The general arrangement would thus well correspond
with the well-known front of Abbaye aux Hommes, Caen, for which
see plate in App. to Vol. I. of Storer's *Cathedrals*.

* The insertion of windows in this position originated in the fact
that until quite lately there existed here examples of late three-light
Decorated windows. They appear in Hollar's views as well as in
Dickenson's. The one in the north-west tower was removed and
replaced by a blank window-arch of Norman character in 1801-2,
when it was thought necessary to strengthen the tower. This was
pierced for glazing *c.* 1850, when the Decorated window in the south
tower was also removed. The tracery of the latter, an exceedingly
beautiful example of double-foliated tracery of the reticulated pattern, described by Mr. Freeman in his *Window Tracery*, is preserved
in one of the gardens attached to the vicarage. By the kind permis-
sion of the lady who now occupies the garden I have been able to
obtain a photograph of the tracery, and from it is made the rough
sketch which appears in one of our plates. It appears in its original
position in a plate in Clarke and Killpack's *Southwell*, published in
1838. The weather-course on the north-west tower cannot be explained. Hollar's view shews a tall canopy-shaped shed over a small
doorway between the west doorway and the near buttress of the same
tower. The shed was removed and the doorway blocked in 1771.

feature which first suggested the Early English pointed arch, but it is now generally believed to have had a purely constructive origin.

The West Door.

There is no part of their churches upon which the Normans bestowed more pains than their doorways. They were often composed of a succession of receding arches, and to gain depth of wall in which to build them a sort of flat buttress was applied to the main wall. Malmesbury Abbey has a portal of eight such arches. In the case before us there are five: four of them spring from detached jamb-shafts with ornamented capitals, and in their arch-mouldings the common zigzag alternates with a filleted edge-roll; while the fifth and innermost arch, continued without impost to the ground, is enriched with a more beautiful variety of zigzag. A dripstone of double-billet moulding surmounts the whole. The tyro in architecture must notice the square plinth-stones and abaci, and the scolloped capitals of the shafts—characteristic features of Norman work. Now let us pass to the south side of the church.

Nave Aisles: Exterior.

There is only one of the original Norman windows of the nave now left, the westernmost window of the *north* aisle; the round-headed windows in the first three bays of the south aisle are good copies of it. The inferior order of the arch consists of a moulding of zigzag running down the jambs without impost; above this is a large edge-roll springing from detached jamb-shafts; and the whole is surmounted by a dripstone of the double-billet. The square abacus is continued along the wall as a string-course, which dies away into the buttress. The three windows were inserted *c.* 1847.* At that time an Early English chapel, occupying the second bay and projecting outwards, was pulled down.† The original Norman windows were replaced in early Perpendicular times by windows like those still occupying the last four bays of the aisle. Similar insertions still remain in the north aisle. ' Though the general character of the Norman work suffers from their presence, yet we would in no wise have them removed, since they preserve to us an important feature of the history of the fabric. The dripstones terminate in sculptures of the heads of females with the square head-dress worn in the reign of Richard II.‡ Here we may notice again the horizontal string-courses. The continuity of the lower one of zigzag, which once ran right along immediately under the sills of the Norman windows, is now broken by the Perpendicular windows. It is curious to remark how, when the latter were inserted, the displaced portions of the string-course were simply removed to the

* Before this restoration was made the first bay had a plain Norman doorway with single jamb-shafts, and above it a window like the other original aisle-windows, but somewhat smaller.

† Called Booth's chapel, because Abp. Lawrence Booth added to it and founded therein two fresh chantries. Mr. Dimock tells us that the first chapel was in all likelihood built by Canon Henry le Vavasour, who founded a chantry at the altar of S. John Baptist, 1275-1280: and with regard to its destruction, he adds—Thoroton speaks of it as having become in his time, "by negligence in the late wars and since," utterly ruinous. It was afterwards repaired, and used as a school and library, but was taken down in 1784. The arch of communication into the nave aisle, in the second bay from the west tower, was visible until within a few years; it was of late Early English character, and was walled up, with an atrocious window of three lights. In removing the old foundation of this part of the aisle, some five years since (i.e. *c.* 1847), previous to underpinning, the whole walling-up fell in. The bay was thereupon restored, according to the Norman arrangement.

‡ Mr. Dimock remarks that these windows are really late Decorated work, the mouldings having a close similarity to those of the window described in the preceding note.

lower level of the new window-sills, the break being filled up
vertically with the mouldings which came from the jambs of
the destroyed Norman windows.   The architect will at once
detect the difference in the sections of the two kinds of zigzag.
Just above the upper string-course is a series of small square
windows which give light to the triforium, which is not,
therefore, in this case a blind-story.   Above this again we
come to one of the most peculiar features of the whole building—I mean the clerestory of circular windows, perfectly
plain, without cuspings.   There is no parallel to this now
existing in England.   At Ledbury, indeed, in Herefordshire,
there is a clerestory of circular lights, but the roofs of the
aisles have been raised above them on the outside, so that they
can be seen only from the interior of the church. ' Circular
Norman windows, without tracery, also occur in the chapter-
house of Oxford Cathedral, and in Canterbury Cathedral.
At Gretton Church, in Leicestershire, the clerestory has
plain circular and triangular windows alternating, but this
belongs to a later date.   It only remains to notice the plain
nebule corbel-tables, which support parapet walls, running
along above the aisle and clerestory windows.   The parapets
are not Norman, either here or on the lantern tower, for
the original roofs had projecting eaves coming down just
over the corbel-tables which supported them, like the present western spires, but of course without any cant.   The
present high-pitched roofs are a recent restoration by Mr.
Christian.   The parapets were doubtless built when the
original eave-roofs were lowered throughout, possibly in the
15th century at the time when the large west window was
inserted.   The old low-pitched roofs appear in Hollar's views
of 1672, and must have been renewed after the fire destroyed
them in 1711.

Transepts : Exterior.

The windows in the second stage of the transept are worth
notice. The arch shews a curious example of cable-moulding,
which occurs again in a much bolder form in the interior in
the great arches supporting the lantern tower. The dripstone
is composed of three overhanging rows of a small square-
footed nebule. In the south wall of the south transept there
is a fine segmental doorway, of which the jamb-shafts and
their caps were restored c. 1847. It is worthy of notice that
the zigzag string-course, already mentioned as running all
round the Norman church, rises over this doorway, forming a
hood or dripstone.* The pitch of the old low roofs may be
clearly seen in the restored gables of the transepts. These
heavy gables, without relief of windows and with their peculiar ornamentation, are very remarkable : the pattern of the
ornamentation in the two transepts is similar in character but
different in treatment, the parts indented in the one being
embossed in the other. A close examination of the parapet
wall of the lantern tower will shew that in it are worked up
many stones having precisely the ornamentation so peculiar
in the gables, and a cursory glance will shew that the work-
manship of the corner pinnacles is very similar; moreover
these pinnacles, each consisting of a cylindrical shaft with
conical capping, are very like the somewhat plainer pinnacles
which flank the gable of the north porch, as we shall presently
see. The conclusion drawn from this is that the removal of
the pyramidal roof of the tower and the lowering of the nave
and transepts roofs took place at the same time, and that the
parapet was built partly of the stones which came from the
destroyed gables, and that the corner pinnacles came from the

---

* Quite recently an inserted doorway of no merit was removed
from the corresponding position in the north transept.

same place. As Mr. Dimock remarks, placed on the corners
of the transept gables, in correspondence with the similar and
similarly-situated pinnacles of the north porch, they would
be in good place and good proportion; whereas now they only
strike the eye as repugnant to the Norman arrangement of a
tower, and injurious in their comparative dwarfishness to the
massive character of the structure on which they stand.

I have fully discussed the features of the east wall of the
south transept in Chapter III.* The clearly marked gable-
moulding shews the pitch of the roof of a semi-circular
apsidal chapel which belonged to the Norman church. There
were originally three other apses, one annexed to the corresponding wall of the north transept, and one at the east end of
each choir aisle, while the chancel had a square termination.
Romsey Church, Hants, has similar apsidal chapels to the
transepts, as well as two others worked into the main wall at
the corners of the chancel. Circular chapels may be seen,
too, varying in form, at Tewkesbury Abbey, at Gloucester,
Norwich, and Canterbury Cathedrals, and elsewhere. At
Peterborough they have been destroyed. Another gable-
moulding, on the east side of the lantern tower, shews the
pitch of the roof of the old Norman choir, and if we follow
the corbel-table of the transept to its juncture with the tower
we see it continued two or three feet on the return wall of
the clerestory of the present choir.

---

* It was agreed in chapter, August 12th, 1784, to build a new
library, running eastwards from this wall. The records contain the
following marginal note by the hand of Archdeacon Wilkins:—
"A pretty piece of business this, by which the beautiful lancet
"windows of the south aisle of the choir were bricked up and a large
"lean-to made for a library-room, with a chimney against the said
"windows, and other incongruous adjuncts—all happily pulled down,
"and the foundations and walls underpinned, the windows and walls
"restored to their primitive form by me. G. W.—A.D. 1847." It
was in reality pulled down in 1825, long before this note was written.

The Choir: Exterior.—South-East View.

In passing from the Norman to the Early English part of the church we are sorry to have to introduce our remarks with another lamentation. The light and lofty character of the Early English style, as contrasted with the low massive look of the Norman, has been in a great measure destroyed by the lowering throughout of the high-pitched roofs. On the east side of the tower again we can still see the weather-course of the original choir-roof, running up almost to the top of the arcading which adorns its second stage; and on the clerestory wall is the mark of the old roof of the secondary transepted chapels which occupy the fifth bay of the choir. This, however, is a loss which we may hope the architect will see his way to restoring to us, and we have in what remains an example of the style which in refinement and delicacy is hardly surpassed. "The noble choir," wrote Sir Gilbert Scott, "seems to be an emanation from Lincoln."* It certainly reminds one very much of the nave and transept of that noble building, and its date is very little later. The treatment of the buttresses and base-mouldings is very similar in the two buildings, and the similarity is seen in other details. The deep projection of the buttresses contrasts with the broad shallow pilasters of the Norman period—the comparative thinness of the Early English walls requiring much greater support. They are square in the lower stage, and largely chamfered above, terminating in heavy acute triangular heads with sunken faces and adorned with dog-tooth, which rise up through the parapet wall. Had the aisles their original eave-roofs, these triangular heads would stand up much more prominently than they do now—much as they do in the but-

* *Mediæval Architecture.*

tresses of the chancel. For the benefit of the young student
we may remark that the dog-tooth is as characteristic an
ornament of this style as the ball-flower is of the following
one: it is described as a small pyramid cut into four leaves
which meet at the apex. The deep under-cutting of the bold
base-mouldings and string-courses is equally characteristic.
The windows are single-lancets, with the glazing deeply set
and with largely chamfered jambs—generally a pair in each
bay, with a continuous dripstone, the arches springing from
single shafts, engaged and filleted. The parapet above the
clerestory is original and very fine: it is carried on a corbel-
table of grotesque heads, with two courses of cornice mouldings enriched with dog-tooth and a plain face between them.
The two flying buttresses with crocketed pinnacles are Decorated work, c. 1355, probably, built no doubt to counteract
damage threatened by the great weight of the roof and by
the outward thrust of the heavy stone vaulting in the interior.
It is a pity they were ever found necessary, for, without being
specially good examples of the style, they mar the harmony
of the Early English work besides breaking the continuity of
the elegant clerestory. But in some of our larger churches,
when a whole series of flying buttresses spanning the aisles
is seen, as at Gloucester or Howden, it forms a striking
feature in the general view. The western one of these
two, until a recent restoration, had a water-drain running
down its ridge and issuing through the lower part of the
pinnacle in front. Mr. Petit has preserved it in a drawing
published in the Lincoln volume of the *Proceedings of the
Arch. Inst.* It was in a dangerous state, and in restoration
it was thought safer to rebuild it like its neighbour. Before
going round to the east front the visitor may get a fine south-
east view of the church by passing along the wall of the
Palace towards the corner of the church-yard: it was from a

point under this wall that Turner took his sketch of the
minster, and in following his taste and judgment I suppose
no one can err.

East Front.

The choir-aisles consist of six bays, their east walls containing each a pair of lancets, and beyond projects a chancel of
two bays. The east front of the chancel, like that of York,
is square and runs up to the full height of the main building.
Bold, massive buttresses stand in rectangular pairs at the
corners, and each pair is surmounted with an octagonal pinnacle. Each pinnacle has shafts at its angles, which support
an acute gablet over each of its faces. From within the
gablets rises a small ribbed spire, terminating in a bunch of
crocketed foliage. Above the lower blank stage the east front
has two tiers of lancets, four of equal height in each. The
lower tier fills the whole space between the buttresses, while
in the upper tier, the lancets being narrower, there is an
additional blank arch between them and the buttress on each
side. The lancets are separated by triple-clustered shafts
supporting arches of two orders enriched with dog-tooth, and
they are combined under a continuous dripstone similarly
enriched. The combination of four lancets of equal height
in the east front of Southwell presents a peculiarity of which
there is, I believe, no parallel instance extant. The form
usually adopted by Early English builders is a triplet of lancets, the middle one being higher than the others, while a
quintette, in which the height rises in gradation to the centre
one, is found in two or three of our churches. Four combined
lancets, however, may be seen in Repton Church, and in
Trinity Hospital Chapel, Leicester; but in each case the two
middle windows are higher than the outside ones. Of course
"the wretched battlemented low gable," with its miserable

erushed window, is not original. The cross which crowned the gable it replaced once rose far above the tops of the flanking pinnacles. It is only necessary to stand before the transepts of Lincoln or York to imagine how great a loss the east front has suffered by the lowering of the choir roof, and we cannot express too strong a hope that its ancient beauty will ere long be restored. I think there can be little doubt that the opinion that the old gable contained a circular window is erroneous. The windows throughout the Early English work are of a decidedly early character, uniformly plain without a sign of tracery. Moreover had there been a circular window here, we should expect to find the same in the half-gables of the east fronts of the aisles, as in the case of the transept with its side-aisles at Beverley. But there we have lancets, and here, too, there must have been an arcading of lancet arches, probably seven in all, their height increasing towards the centre one, and one or two of them pierced for glazing to give light to the space between the interior ceiling and the roof above. The five sisters of York have an arcading of seven lancet arches above them. At the east end of Ely there are seven above five in the main aisle, and in the side-aisles five above a triplet. This was in fact the common arrangement. The eastern elevation of Whitby Abbey, now in ruins, bears the closest resemblance in design to Southwell east front: the gable there contains as many as seven lancets above a triplet only.

The Chapter-House and Vestibule: Exterior.

The chapter-house is a necessary adjunct to all conventual churches, whether secular or monastic. Secular canons, living, as they did, in the world like other people, had no common dormitory and often-times no cloister attached to their church, but they wanted a common room in which they

might meet to discuss and transact the business of their college, and this room, the chapter-house in fact, was in their
foundations always closely connected with the church, having
in most instances no entrance but from the interior of the
church. In monastic foundations, on the contrary, the
chapter-house was not more closely connected with the church
than the other common buildings, which were arranged round
a cloister generally attached to the south nave-aisle and transept; and in it the monks, both lay and clerical, used to meet
daily to read a portion (called *capitulum* or little chapter) of
the rule under which they lived. In secular churches the
chapter house is more often found on the north side of the
church, and east of the transept, as at Southwell. In Norman
times the chapter-house was generally a rectangular building,
as at Durham, Gloucester, and Bristol: but the beautiful
series of examples of the 13th century assumed a polygonal
shape. With Southwell we may compare Lincoln, Salisbury
(on south of church), Wells, and Westminster.

In the preceding chapters I have had occasion to speak of
the great similarity of the York and Southwell chapter-houses,
drawing the conclusion that they were designed by the same
hand. The building before us belongs to the style called
Decorated, and to that early division of it which synchronizes
roughly with the reign of the first Edward, and is called
Geometrical from the form of the tracery of the windows.
The windows here are of three lights, having circles, both
trefoiled and quatrefoiled, in the heads. They are large and
well-proportioned, in this respect contrasting favourably with
the smaller lights of the preceding style. In fact with each
succeeding style of architecture the size of the windows
increased, and this assumed an exaggerated form when architectural art began to degenerate in Perpendicular times. In
plan the chapter-house is a regular octagon, with a vestibule

attached to its western face. The buttresses at the angles are massive and of great projection. They are divided by string-courses into three stages, the uppermost stage of each having a niche in its face, once filled with a figure. Above this the buttress terminates in a gablet adorned with crockets and finials. From the back of each gablet, again, there rises through the parapet a lofty square pedestal carrying a crocketed pinnacle. The pinnacles have at some period been badly patched up. This pedestal is ribbed at the corners, and each of its faces, which are sunk concavely, terminates in a trefoil within a gablet crocketed and finialed. Four grotesque figures project horizontally from the corners of the pedestal at the points where the gablets spring from the ribs. The high-pitched roof is a recent restoration. The design of the parapet is exquisite, and though rich it has some early details —a corbel-table, for instance, is seldom found in the Decorated style (but cp. Weston-upon-Welland, Northamptonshire, *late*), while the pierced part is generally of a more wavy character. The corbel-table is a series of trefoiled arches springing from heads, and the spandrels also are trefoiled; above this there is a hollow cornice-moulding filled with a row of dog-tooth of the late leafy kind; then comes a broad plain face; and this is surmounted by a series of pierced quatrefoils. It only remains to notice that some of the crockets of the gablets and pinnacles are of the early form like a bishop's *crook*, from which the crocket is said to derive its name,* and that in the western wall of the vestibule there is an instance of an ogee-arched window.

---

* More commonly derived from Fr. *croc*. But there is in M.E. literature a word *crok*, a crook or hook, of which our *crocket* is probably merely the diminutive. The corresponding word in Fr. architecture is *crochet*, from *croc*, which itself is a word of Teutonic origin.

The North Transept Chapel: Exterior.

Between the vestibule and the north transept we have the exterior wall of an Early English chapel, built very shortly after the completion of the choir. The beautiful arcade of lancets in the middle stage, pierced in two instances for lights, is as purely Early English in character as anything we have in the choir, The tracery of the lower window is of course a much later insertion, and the low-gabled parapet and the flanking-gabled heads of the Early English buttresses also seem to point to a somewhat later date. On the other side of this gable, as may be seen from the top of the lantern tower, there is the weather-moulding of a slanting roof running down just above the three-light window. There is no doubt that the upper part of this building was originally left in quite an unfinished state. It is difficult to assign exact dates to the gable and the depressed window it contains. Mr. Dimock thought that at any rate the window (though not its tracery) was Early English work, arguing, I think, from the presence of the dog-tooth. But compare this ornament with the dog-tooth in the triangular head of the Early English buttress hard by, and you will find it quite different. In fact it is a plain-faced pyramid, more like the nail-head than the dog-tooth. The buttresses are much like those of the choir already described, but in the third stage the chamfered edges of the lower stages slope up to a point, a feature which seems to enhance their beauty.*

---

* Many years ago the monster which now crowns the gable of the north transept was lying in the workshop of Mr. Ingleman, builder, whence it was removed to Upton Hall. It found yet another home before being reclaimed and placed, quite lately, in the position which it probably originally occupied.

The North Porch.

Though the Normans bestowed special pains on the enrichment of their doorways, yet Norman porches are somewhat rare: the one at Malmesbury Abbey, Wilts., is perhaps one of the finest we have. The instance before us is almost unique in having an upper-room. The outer arch consists of two orders, moulded and springing from engaged semi-cylindrical shafts, with capitals scolloped and otherwise ornamented. The zigzag string-course already noticed as running round the Norman church forms the abacus and is carried along the interior walls above an arcade of intersecting arches, the bases of which rest on a stone bench on each side. The inner doorway consists of a series of six receding arches, most of them having some variety of the zigzag moulding, springing from detached jamb-shafts. The innermost arch springs from its jambs without imposts, as in the west doorway, while the order next above shews what is called the beak-head moulding. The oak doors themselves are worth notice: the panels, which are covered with flowing Decorated tracery, are not framed but cut out of the solid wood. The ceiling of the porch is a plain barrel vault of rubble-work, originally intended to receive the plaster. The plaster was removed some time since, and the effect is doubtless better without it. The gable above the outer archway contains three beautiful round-headed windows, which give light to the chamber within, the middle one being taller than the others. They are similar in detail to the original windows of the nave. There is a separate dripstone over each, consisting of the triple nebule and terminating in long grotesque heads. A row of square heads, similar to those under the eaves of the roofs of the towers, support the parapets on the side walls of the porch. The gable in the front is flanked by cylindrical

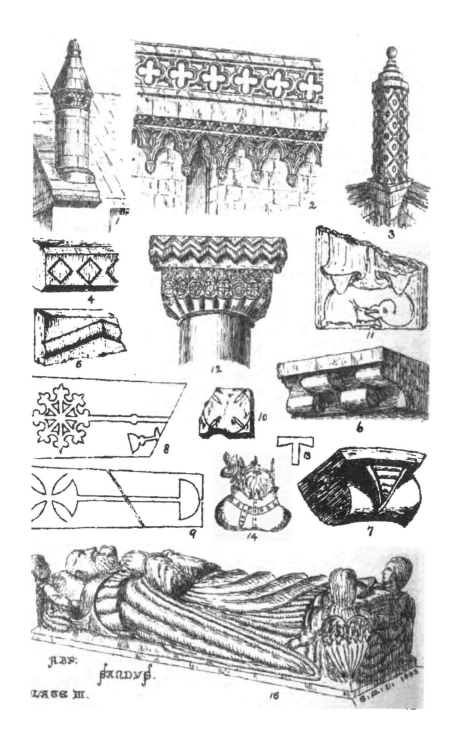

ADP: SANDYS.
LATE III.

turrets, similar in form to those now on the corners of the lantern, but plainer in design. The western one is a peculiar example of a Norman chimney, with holes pierced round the top for the exit of the smoke. The fireplace within was formerly removed, but the lintel has been lately found and restored to its place. The chamber is entered by a doorway which communicates with the triforium, and on either side in the thickness of the wall there is a square recess for a cupboard. It was doubtless meant for a living-room. In some instances such rooms, which are not uncommon over porches of the Decorated and Perpendicular styles, were inhabited by recluses, men who, expressing a determination to separate themselves altogether from the world, were shut in with some ceremony, and the door sealed up. But in these cases there was always some small window or other opening through which means of sustenance might be received by the votary into his cell, and the absence of such an opening in this case precludes the possibility of the room having ever been a reclusorium. Perhaps a sacrist lived here, for the records make mention of a sacrist who should lie within the church, to be at hand to ring the bells at the appointed hours. The Norman porch at Bredon Church, Worcester, has a room over it. Sherborne Abbey affords another example, shewing, however, some additional 15th century work upon it. These are, I believe, the only other instances of a Norman porch with an upper-room of the same date. The room over the porch at Witney, Oxfordshire, is a later addition.

The Nave: Interior.

Entering the Minster by the west door we may begin by pausing to take a full-length view of the nave. I am not prepared to bestow unqualified praise upon the design and

arrangement of the Norman interior. It is impossible to be
enthusiastic about the long, low, bare clerestory wall, scarcely
relieved by the small round arches which admit the light from
windows which cannot be seen; or about the triforium arcade,
which seems far too massive for its low elevation. There is a
certain depressing sense of lowness which is especially felt
when one looks at the elevation of each bay separately. But
we have to remember that this lowness is one of the characteristic features of Norman design, and to guard against
drawing comparisons in this respect with buildings of later
date, when the use of the pointed arch enabled them to be
carried to so much greater heights. And there is a massive
grandeur about the whole which the rudeness of the design
and the simplicity of the ornamentation seems to enhance.
The horizontal lines dividing the stages carry the eye along
the building past a succession of vast solid piers until it rests
in the distance upon the bold and lofty arch of the lantern
tower, which with its boldness and great height seems to
redeem the faults in design which would be so striking without it. And the grandeur of the general effect is insured by
the high-pitched semi-circular ceiling* with which Mr. Christian has replaced the late wretched flat ceiling. It is, perhaps,
a pity that the view of the succession of curved braces of
which it is framed had to be broken by the immense square
tie-beams which span the breadth of the nave; but, when we
think of the great weight of the solid carpentry of the ceiling
and of the fact that the strength of the clerestory walls is
much lessened by the gallery that runs within them, it is at
once seen that they were a necessary precaution.

* The original Norman ceilings must have been of much the same
form as the present nave ceiling—perhaps they were slightly canted.
The series of folio-sized lithographic views of the minster, by Buckler,
shews the nave with its former flat ceiling—they are well worth the
small amount which will buy them, and the more so since the letter-
press was written specially for them by Mr. Dimock.

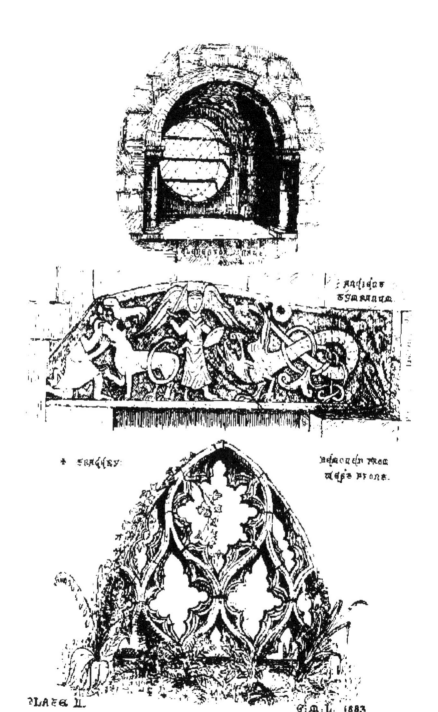

CHESTER RACE

RADIDAS
SYMANNA

✠ SRAGHSY

RAFACH IN MEE
NESS FFONE

PLATE II.   G. M. L. 1883

The cylindrical piers of the nave arcade are about 4½ ft. in thickness and only 19 ft. in height; the bases are square, and the abaci, as at Tewkesbury, Gloucester, and Malmesbury, are round, and the capitals variously ornamented. The arch consists of two orders with a hood-mould of the double billet: the inferior order shews an uncommon variety of a common moulding—a square keel set diamond-wise between two edge-rolls—which occurs in the tower of the somewhat earlier building of S. Alban's Abbey; the superior order has a broad plain soffit with an edge-roll flanked on the face by a filleted hollow. The triforium stage contains a gallery the full width of the aisle below. The arches of the arcade are of the same span as those just described, but of much less height; here the abaci are square, the two orders of each arch spring from semi-cylindrical shafts with scolloped cushion capitals, and the hood-moulds consist of a small triple-nebule. There is a peculiarity here which must not pass unnoticed since it bears witness to the fact that the Norman builders felt that the broad span of these low massive arches wanted some relief, while it shews that they failed to carry out their original design in this stage. Each arch has three curious projecting stones, one at the crown and one at each spring of the inferior order. They are explained by the existing arrangement of the triforium of Romsey Abbey, Hants., where the main arch is divided by a central shaft, which carries two subordinate arches and an upright which rises from the impost to the crown of the larger arch above.* The small plain arches which break the blank wall of the clerestory stage, so unattractive from the floor of the nave, with the passage and

---

* The architect recently inserted the framework of such an arrangement in one of the arches, to see the effect, but determined to leave the arcade in its present form.

circular lights within them, become more attractive when
seen from their own level. A sketch of one of them appears
in Plate II.*

Nave Aisles: Interior.

The aisles afford an example of a fine quadripartite vaulted
ceiling, the groin-ribs of which have a moulding similar to
that of the inferior order of the nave arches, except that they
have a double instead of a single diamond keel between the
rolls. The ribs of this heavy stone vault spring simply from
corbels in the wall. The transverse arches are very much
stilted, in fact they are almost horse-shoe in form. The key-
stones at the intersections of the cross-ribs are generally plain,
but that under the north-west tower is sculptured with a
grotesque double head. The walls of the aisles have no
arcading, so common in the richer buildings of this style;
there is simply a stone bench running along the foot. In the
first bay of the north aisle remains the one original nave
window: the rere-arch has a continuous edge-roll and filleted
hollow, the jambs are largely splayed, and the sill ascends in
steps to the glazing. In the wall of the second bay on the
same side is a recess with a semi-circular but late Early
English arch containing a slab of Purbeck marble with a
beautiful raised cross upon it. The slab doubtless covers the
remains of the founder of a chantry chapel erected here.
Moreover, when the whitewash was removed (o. 1850) the
vaulting of this bay, and this bay only, shewed signs of having
been at one time enriched with painting. The space between
the piers of the easternmost bay but one on the south side is
the site of another of the numerous chantry chapels in this

---

*†See similar sketch by Mr. Petit in the Lincoln Vol. of the Journal
of the Arch. Inst.

church; the eastern pier shews marks of a sculpture of the Virgin and the Lily now destroyed.*

Lantern Tower and Transepts: Interior.

The lantern tower is supported by four lofty arches opening into the four arms of the cross. It is curious that the span of the transept arches is greater than the span of the arch opening into the nave. This arrangement, while leaving the transepts comparatively free and open, at the same time allows the responds of the western arch to project considerably beyond the lines of the nave arcades, whereby the boldness of its appearance from the west end of the nave is rendered more striking. The responds of this arch, and of its eastern companion, consist of three semi-cylindrical shafts, from which the three orders of the arches spring. The responds of the two remaining arches are single semi-cylindrical shafts of the same diameter as the piers of the nave arcade. The middle order of each arch is a bold cable-moulding. It differs from the plain-twisted cable often used by classical and Norman architects, an example of which may be seen at Romsey. Each coil is distinctly keeled round its broadest part, and the whole looks like a series of double cones arranged spirally—another ingenious device to enhance its effect when seen from a distance. In the interior of the tower, in the first stage above the great arches, there are eight richly ornamented arches, two in each wall. In former times they were quite hidden from view by the flat ceilings. They open into a gallery or passage running round the tower, and across this, through corresponding arches in the exterior faces

* See next chapter.—Standing near one of the pillars a little lower down on the same side (the fifth from the west, I think it is), one catches a beautiful glimpse of the north transept chapel, the light streaming through the flowing tracery of its windows.

of the walls, into the four arms of the church. The old low-pitched roofs ran diagonally across them, allowing the upper portions of them to be seen from the outside of the building. The stage above this is adorned with similar arches, through which, across another gallery, the lantern windows throw their light into the interior of the tower. These arches are now partly hidden by the wooden gallery used by the bell-ringers, which unfortunately became a necessity when the flat ceiling was removed. Perhaps the bells will some day be placed in the western towers. A drawing by Coney, published in the last edition* of the *Monasticon*, shews the interior of the lantern tower to great advantage.

The transepts are at once bold in design and rich in detail. The south transept is perhaps the more beautiful. The cable-moulding is used in the window-arches of the middle stage with fine effect, and the triple nebule prevails largely. There is a remarkable irregularity in the cable-moulding of one of the windows in the western wall. The windows of the lower stage are similar to the original nave window already described, but to carry off the greater thickness of the wall they are enriched with an additional order. The east and west walls of the transept contain a passage which is continued round the end wall also; but in this case it is not in the thickness of the wall, but carried by a fine pair of arches with a projection of 2 ft. Perhaps it was thought that the end wall, having to carry a heavy gable, required extra strength; but other Norman buildings, Winchester for instance, do not shew a like precaution in like case. The arches span the transept and spring from corbels at the sides and at the centre from a cylindrical shaft, the capital of which is worth notice. They are ornamented with a double row of cable, twisted in oppo-

---

* Caley, Ellis, and Blandinel, 1817-30.

site directions. In the eastern wall of the transept there still remains the large arch of entrance into the semi-circular chapel long since destroyed. The chapel has been fully discussed in the foregoing chapter. The arch shews on the edge of its superior order a good example of zigzag, and has an inferior order of a double row of cable partly hidden. In the stage above there is a bold arcade of three arches, which may originally have communicated with the upper story of the apsidal chapel. Lofty plain arches communicate with the nave and choir aisles, and above them, through very similar arches, the triforia open out into the transept. The braces of the wooden ceiling are not barrel-formed as in the nave ceiling, but canted.

The north transept presents nearly the same features as the south. Here, however, the destroyed apsidal chapel has been replaced by one of Early English date, which we shall consider later on. A description of the sculpture over the belfry doorway, of the effigy of Abp. Sandys, both in this transept, as well as of the capitals of the piers of the eastern lantern-tower arch, will be found in the next chapter. In this arch, on its eastern side, as well as in the northern arch on the transept side, the cable-moulding is replaced by a large roll with a plain square moulding above it. In the wall above the effigy of Abp. Sandys there is a fragment of zigzag string-course which must not pass unnoticed, no similar moulding occurring elsewhere in the church.

The Choir: Interior.

It was but little more than a century after the completion of the Norman church when its choir was pulled down to be rebuilt on a much larger scale, in the less massive but more elegant style which prevailed in the 13th century. Doubtless

it was felt that the small Norman choir, which was not so
much as half the length of its successor, was unsuited to the
high position which the church of Southwell held in the
diocese of York.   Probably it was found practically inconvenient.   It was large enough for the daily use of the fifty or
sixty persons, maybe, belonging to the college, but Southwell
was more than a collegiate church, it was the mother church
of the county of Nottingham; and when at the annual synod
all the clergy and a great number of the laity of the county
went in procession to present their offerings and attend divine
service, it would be filled to overflowing.   The plan adopted
in the erection of the new choir can be fairly clearly traced.
That the Norman choir extended only to the middle of the
fourth bay of the present one has been proved by an examination of the foundations.   It was left standing until the
whole of the new work lying east of it was completed.   This
is proved by the fact that the foundations of the eastern half
of the choir are composed entirely of a stone found in the
immediate neighbourhood; while in the foundations of the
western part, which occupies the site of the old choir, inter-
mixed with the local stone there is a large quantity of stone
like that which the Normans used in those portions of their
church which remain standing now.   The Early English
builders obtained their stone from Mansfield, and it is a light
sandstone with blue veins in it.   The Normans used a darker
sandstone, of a yellowish hue, found at Mansfield Woodhouse.
The whole of the eastern part of the choir is built of the
light coloured stone, while in the western and later part the
darker stone is used together with the light.   In fact the
Early English builders, when they reached the Norman choir,
pulled it down and made use of the material in raising the
building which took its place.   It may be further noticed that
in the fourth bay on each side there are irregularities which

denote that here there is a juncture of two works. The crown of the arch on the south side is not so high as that of its fellows, and the space between it and the string-course above is filled in with a curious medallion. On the other side there is an irregularity in the string-course itself. It seems that the builders worked from the east, and when they reached the Norman choir they did not continue their work in the same direction, but began again at the west end of the choir,* and on coming to their old work found their measurements slightly wrong, and corrected their mistake as best they could. Some architectural details confirming this view will be noticed in their place.

Southwell affords no study of the transition from the Norman style to the Early English. The latter flourished from about 1190 to 1270. S. Hugh's choir at Lincoln is the earliest as well as one of the purest examples of Gothic we have, closely followed by the beautiful Galilee of Ely. Then come the excellent choir and transepts of Rochester, the nave and transepts of Lincoln, and the west front of Wells. These are followed by Salisbury, which, from its singular complete-ness, has been called the type of the style. So that Southwell, which was commenced when the choir only of Salisbury had been finished, and is of nearly the same date as the north transept of York, was built when the style was well advanced. It shews in its details many evidences of its somewhat late date, though it has not the profusion of ornament displayed in such buildings as Westminster Abbey and in the later and more beautiful presbytery of Lincoln called the Angels' Choir. In a building of this date we should have expected some approach to division of lights in the windows, instead of the

---

* The abutment of the Early English arcade upon the Norman responds has been considered in the foregoing chapter, pp. 59, 60.

plain single lancets; but the fillets on all the shafts, the plain
round mouldings (without hollows) of many of the bases, and
the longitudinal rib of the vaulting, are one and all signs of
the advance of the style.

The base-mouldings of the piers and responds shew considerable diversity of treatment. Many of them consist of
two rounds and a filleted hollow between, others of three
plain rounds. The hollow, which would hold water, is characteristic of the Early English style, and its absence is generally
a sign of advanced date. All four responds shew the hollow
moulding; it is absent from the bases of five out of six of the
piers in the western or later half of the choir, and from only
one out of four in the eastern part. The piers are octofoil,
composed, that is, of eight clustered shafts, and these are all
filleted. Deep-set between each pair of shafts the responds
shew additional detached shafts banded midway. The pillars
of earlier buildings are often composed entirely of detached
banded shafts, arranged round a central column, as in the
choir at Salisbury. The responds of the arches of the
secondary transepts are also octofoil, and in this case the
smaller shafts are banded. The capitals are of the inverted-
bell shape usual in this style. The arches, with their rounds
and deep hollows, give further evidence of the advance of the
style, since the outline of their mouldings does not sufficiently
conform to the octofoil shape of the piers and capitals from
which they spring. The dog-tooth with which the second
order is enriched is peculiar in that it is worked upon a broad
projecting fillet instead of being placed in a hollow as it
usually is. In the three eastern arches on the south side it
does not appear, a filleted round taking its place. I myself
prefer the latter arrangement, with the bolder effect of light
and shade that it gives, and venture to think the dog-tooth in
this case no gain in beauty of design.

The arrangement of the triforium, clerestory, and vaulting, is very uncommon and very striking. All our large churches of early date have three distinct stages: the arcade separating the side-aisle from the nave or choir ; the triforium, which the architect is free to adorn as he thinks fit; and the clerestory stage. The vaulting-shafts generally run up the wall of the triforium stage, between the bays, to the string-course which separates it from the clerestory above, and at this level the vaulting-ribs spring from them. In this case, however, in building an Early English choir on to a low Norman tower, to preserve the symmetry of the whole internally as well as externally, it was necessary to make the elevation of the choir not so great as we find it in most of our large churches of this style. The architect did not choose to lessen the height and span of the arches of the great arcade, or to build a flat ceiling. He chose rather to make the vault spring from a lower level than is usual, in fact only two or three feet above the top of the lower stage, and practically robbed himself of his triforium stage by merging it into the clerestory stage above, with an effect as pleasing as it is singular. It was doubtless the pleasing effect of this ingenious combination of triforium and clerestory into one stage at Southwell which prompted the adoption, some fifty years later, of a similar arrangement in the Decorated nave of York Minster. It may have become common in Perpendicular times, but we only find two other instances of it in churches as old as Southwell. One occurs in the contemporaneous Early English choir of Pershore Abbey, Worcestershire, and the second in the late Norman church at Steyning, Sussex. To return to Southwell, above the pier arcade each bay contains a pair of lofty lancet arches, which run right up close under the cross vault of the stone vaulting. The arches are very acute and enriched with dog-tooth, and they spring from a tall slender triple-clustered pillar in the middle and corresponding engaged pillars at the sides. The shafts are filleted, and the hollows between them enriched with dog-tooth, like the arch-mouldings. The absence of foliage from some of the capitals only serves to enhance its beauty on others. Behind the pillars runs the triforium gallery, and in the wall on the other side of it there are two plain lancet openings into the space under the aisle roof. Above these are the clerestory windows, likewise lancets, on a level with the capitals of the interior lancets, through which they throw their light into the church. The stone vaulting is quadripartite and enriched with dog-tooth, with bosses of foliage at the intersections of the diagonal ribs, and a longitudinal rib. The narrowness of the cellular compartments which admit the light from the clerestory windows serves well to display the beauty of its elliptical curve. The series of short triple-clustered vaulting-shafts, with their rich capitals and the exceptionally fine corbels of stiff-stalked foliage on which they rest, placed low down between the pier arches, form together one of the beautiful features of the choir; they are banded to the wall, as it were, by the deep under-cut string-course which embraces them.

The east windows have already been treated of, but we may here notice that it is the use of the vaulting-shaft and rib of which the longitudinal rib of the vaulting is a continuation which prevented the introduction of a central window. A like arrangement exists at Romsey Abbey and Glasgow Cathedral Church. The present arrangement of the chancel is cramped and undignified. The raised platform on which the altar-table stands occupies only half its area, and the ascent of five steps is sudden and awkward. It is proposed to raise the flooring of the rest of the chancel to the same higher level,

to bring the altar-table further forward,* and to make the
approach more gradual. The first step will be placed between
the fourth piers of the choir arcade, two more between the
fifth piers, and the remaining two between the eastern
responds. Thus the fifth and sixth bays of the choir will
be occupied by ascending platforms on which chairs can
be placed at festivals and on other occasions when an extra
number of sittings is required.†

There is not much to say about the aisles. The ribs of the
quadripartite vaulting spring on the one side from the capitals
of the pier arches, on the other from corbels. There are many
additional ribs springing from vaulting-shafts placed between
the lancets in each bay. Piscinas and aumbries occur in the
eastern bays and in each of the transepts. In the south aisle
there are some fine sedilia. In the wall of the same aisle
there is an inserted Perpendicular doorway, now blocked up,
which originally served as a private entrance from the Palace.
The hood-mould terminates in two heads; the western one is
modern, but its companion affords an instance of the S.S.
collar, which will be described in the next chapter. In the
transept on this side is a sepulchral recess, with a semi-circular
arch, containing the effigy of a priest. At the intersection of
the vaulting ribs in the eastern bay of the north aisle there is

---

* "1791, Jan. 20. Whereas sundry and great inconveniences
"have arisen from the present situation of the screen and altar-table,
"which will be entirely removed by taking down screen and placing
"table further back"—ordered to be done.—Note from records.

† Here I may add that low side stalls are to be placed in the two
western bays of the choir. Stalls in the same position have lately
been removed on account of their shutting out the light of the aisle
windows. They were the work of an Italian artist, one Bernasconi,
of the latter part of last century. All their ornamental work was
composition, sunk into or fastened on the stone; but so well executed
that only the closest examination would reveal its true character.
They are preserved, I believe, in the Museum at Nottingham Castle.
In the early part of this century the aisles were darkened by unsightly
galleries, happily removed.

a singular boss formed of four dragon-heads gnawing a flower in the centre. The other bosses throughout the Early English work are rich examples of the conventional foliage character- istic of the style; but we must except one or two towards the west end of the north aisle, which shew foliage decidedly less conventional—an anticipation of the beautiful natural foliage of the succeeding style, and further evidence of a somewhat late date—notably the boss of oak leaves and acorns in the second bay above the entrance to the chapter-house. The doorway on the west of this entrance leads to the upper story of the north transept chapel. To this chapel let us now proceed.

North Transept Chapel: Interior.

This building is decidedly Early English in character, though some of its details suggest a date closely bordering upon the Decorated era. Following very shortly after the choir it is yet a distinct work. That it was not contemplated when the western and later part of the choir was begun seems proved by the fact that the external string-course of the choir is carried on up to its junction with the Norman transept wall—but this part of the choir, be it remembered, was built from west to east. Two arches of entrance, acutely pointed and unequal in height and span, fill up the Norman entrance arch into the destroyed apse, the jamb of which has been cut back to make room for the smaller one of the two. Their mouldings are like those of the arches of the choir arcade, except that the orders are separated by a round instead of a square, which, according to Mr. Dimock, is a Decorated rather than an Early English arrangement. The triple- clustered shaft which is attached to the middle pillar and runs up on the wall above its capital, terminating in a bracket which once supported a statue, I take to be another Decorated feature. The inequality of the entrance arches is due to the division of the chapel internally into two equal parts by the triple-clustered shafts attached on one side to the east wall, on the other to this pillar. Each part once contained an altar, and the piscinas and anmbries appear in the walls. The quadripartite vault, with its longitudinal rib, the under-cut string-course under the windows, and the mouldings of the bases, some hollow, some round, all bear the closest resemblance to the corresponding features of the choir; while the capitals of the pointed arches shew the characteristic stiff-stalked overhanging foliage. Instead of the fillet so freely used in the choir, the vaulting-shafts, and round mouldings of the pillars of the entrance arches, are moulded to a sharp edge which runs down them in the centre, the edge forming the apex of two ogee curves. Mr. Dimock has applied the term *keeled** to a shaft thus moulded. Besides the pair of triple-clustered vaulting-shafts already mentioned there are other single shafts in the four corners of the chapel. The wall-ribs which spring from them have a peculiar curve which unites them with the arch-mouldings on both east and west walls in the form of a hood-mould to them. The three-light windows are not to be taken as any criterion of the date of the building, for they are insertions of fully a century later. Their tracery is of the form called reticulated, resembling, that is, net-work. Mr. Freeman† thinks they were executed by the same hand as the late Decorated windows already mentioned as having been removed from the west front. In speaking of the vaulted ceiling I have forgotten to

---

* Professor Willis adopted the same term in a different sense, calling the fillet on the centre of a round moulding its *keel*, to distinguish it from the fillets at its sides which separate it from the adjoining mouldings, and which he named *wings*.

† *Origin and Growth of Window Tracery.*

call attention to the fact that the plaster has quite lately been scraped off. I venture to think this should have been left. The stones have never been faced, and they have a very rough look; moreover some of them are of a dark colour and completely honey-combed, and surely they were not meant to be seen. There can be little doubt that plaster was used originally, and very likely it was intended for stenciling. Its restoration would throw out the vaulting-ribs and improve the general effect very much. The doorway in the north choir-aisle, leading to the upper story, is probably an insertion of the same date as the chapel. The arch-mouldings are separated here, too, by a round, while the bases of the jamb-shafts have the hollow moulding. The Early English string-course on the aisle-wall is carefully carried over the arch as a hood, and not simply cut away as it is in the case of the Decorated doorway inserted just beyond this one. As we ascend the staircase within we see on our left the external string-course of the choir. At the top of the steps we see the remains of a destroyed newel, probably Norman, and just above it is a part of a shaft with Norman sculpture on it. Until quite lately the room we have now entered was divided into two apartments by a brick wall, the one being used as a treasury, the other as a lumber-room. The walling has been removed and the room fitted up as a library. The fine wooden ceiling is canted in form like that of the transepts, with the addition in its eastern side of a sky-light of a series of square-headed windows. The windows are all lancets externally, internally trefoiled, except one segmented three-light window high up in the south wall—but it is doubtful whether this is original; its tracery certainly is later work. On the west wall the mark of the gable of the Norman apse is plainly seen. Below it is a small round-headed doorway now blocked up, but in Norman times it communicated with the gallery round the middle stage of the transept. On the north side a small opening into the choir is pierced through the wall low down; the high altar could not be seen through it, and it was no doubt intended to afford means of watching the strangers who visited the church on great occasions. The difference between the dark and the light blue-veined sand-stones, Norman and Early English material respectively, can be easily distinguished in the walls, and many of the stones shew interesting examples of the *banker*-marks* adopted by the masons employed.

There are some points about this building which will prove very interesting to the curious visitor. The chapel, previous to the year 1825, was used as a music school and vicars' vestry. In those days the pointed arches were filled with hoarding, which contained a small door of entrance. The chapel had a stone flooring, the marks of which can be seen on all the pillars and walls, its level being about 9 in. above the sill of the narrow doorway in the south wall. This doorway, which leads into a passage running between the chapel and choir-aisle walls, has lately been restored; but its general character, together with its bevelled sill, which is original, bespeaks a very early date, coeval doubtless with the wall itself. In the year '25 the chapel was fitted up as a library: the stone flooring was removed and three massive brick walls built upon the rubble foundation underneath to support boarding for a new floor on the same level as the transept floor. This boarding was carried through the narrow doorway into the passage. The height of the doorway was considerably raised, a new sill was made (the old one being left *in situ* underneath), and its eastern jamb cut back to make it wider—the new jamb may still be seen in the wall from within the passage. The mixed doorway leading into the passage from the transept,† which had been blocked up, was then re-opened, and the modern and under-doorway inserted. The modern wooden floor and brick walls have been removed. The inner doorway has lately been restored

---

* A *banker-man* is a mason who is employed only at the *bench* (A.S. *baenc*). His work is to prepare the rough stone for the builders.

G   † Described on p. 62.

to its original form, and the rubble foundation of the chapel discovered, shewing the remains of the foundations of the destroyed Norman apse. A few loose pavings, not laid with mortar, on the west side of the chapel, were the only remains of any flooring. The bases of the pillars and vaulting-shafts are on different levels: the bases of the shafts on the east side as well as of that on the north-west corner being 7¼ inches lower than the base of the shaft in the south-west corner and the pillars of the pointed arches. This does not seem hard to account for: while the north and east, that is, the exterior walls of the chapel were being built the Norman apse must have been left standing—a course similar to that adopted in building the choir. Then the builders went to work in the interior, and cut away the northern jamb of the Norman arch and enough of the apse wall to give them room to raise the pointed arches and the adjacent shaft in the south-west corner. Then, when they completed the destruction of the apse, they found they had miscalculated their levels. Then, leaving the floor of course to be laid down afterwards, they finished the south wall of the chapel and raised the vault, turning their attention next to the walls of the upper-story and the staircase leading to it. They seem to have covered it originally with a slanting roof, the marks of which may still be seen both within and without. That this was so soon replaced by another roof* seems to imply that it was only a temporary one. In fact the building was left altogether in an unfinished state, probably from want of funds.† It is doubtful whether any floor was laid down in the chapel below, and it is certain that no vault was built over the staircase, which was therefore left open to the room above, and the doorway at the top of the staircase was left with a very rough appearance. All this was plainly seen a short time back, before the room was fitted up as a library.

There can be little doubt that the passage above-mentioned was intended for a means of communication between the chapel and the choir. It is now blocked midway by a brick wall which helps to support the staircase above. Low down in the aisle-wall, just west of the staircase doorway, there is the lintel of a square-headed inserted doorway, through which

---

* Compare remarks on the exterior of this building, p. 79.

† See remarks on its date, p. 54.

the passage must have opened out into the aisle by means of a short flight of steps. The part of the passage now seen has very lately been opened down to its full depth, and features have been thereby exposed which seem to bear out the suggestion made in Chapter III. (pp. 61, 62) that there was originally a Norman newel staircase here, leading to the upper-room of the apse, like the one which existed in the same position in the old Norman church of York, and the one still existing at Norwich. I propose to follow up the subject here, very briefly discussing its bearing upon the features seen in the junction of the two Early English works. The argument there advanced that the Early English builders did not pierce the Norman transept wall, when they made the mixed* doorway leading into the passage, but found rather a doorway there already and merely widened it, receives confirmation from the peculiar curve *inwards* with which the string-course of the aisle-wall begins. There is one feature which argues against the theory of the newel, which I omitted to notice. I mean the external string-course, a large torus moulding, which appears on the Norman wall facing one as one ascends the library staircase. It is easier to admit this single difficulty, and dismiss it, than to waive in its favour the combination of evidence which argues for the theory. One merely has to assume that the newel staircase was an after-thought in the plan of the Norman church, just as the present staircase was an after-thought in the plan of the Early English builders. The first additional fact to notice is the slope of the ground on which the church is built from west to east. The ground outside is slightly above the level of the floor at the west end of the nave, and going eastwards it drops some feet below the level of the choir floor.† The level of the ground on which the chapel and the adjoining aisle-wall stand is fully three feet below the level of the transept floor. In opening down this passage, then, it is only the level of the ground which has been reached, and the

---

* The Early English mouldings have been renewed, but they are said to be an exact copy of the originals. The Norman work is old material used up as is evident from the joints of the masonry alone; the moulding is an edge-roll with a filleted hollow, and exactly corresponds with the moulding of the rere-arch of the Norman windows; it came probably from one of the windows of the destroyed choir.

† The floor of the nave sinks, that of the choir rises, slightly, from west to east, not enough to affect the argument at all.

Norman masonry exposed above this level, if it were a part of the aisle and transept walls, would shew ashlar-work and a continuation of the base-course which runs along the nave and transepts. But these are absent, and the masonry is evidently the remains of the rough-stone foundation of some building which was on the same level as the transept floor, and occupied the space between the Norman apse and aisle-wall. The rest of the foundations would be worked away by the Early English builders in building the south wall of their chapel and in obtaining space for the passage to run beside it.

The next point to notice here is the absence of any base-course along the Early English aisle-wall in this passage, notwithstanding the fact that an external string-course is seen some feet higher up. Two facts must be remembered, first that this north aisle seems to be later than the south aisle of the choir, and that it was built from west to east. It seems then that, when this wall was built, a part of the newel only was destroyed, and that the plans of the builders with regard to the retention or destruction of the Norman apse were not matured. The "mixed" doorway in the transept wall may be coeval either with the aisle-wall or with the later chapel. If the former, then it must have been intended to retain the apse and repair the newel. If the latter, then the intention must have been to make a new staircase ascend from the transept to the upper-room in place of the destroyed newel,* a project which must have been abandoned almost immediately in favour of the present staircase from the aisle. The doorway of this staircase has been considered by some to be coeval with the aisle-wall and earlier than the chapel. The argument in favour of this lies in the fact that the interior string-course is carried over it as a hood to the arch. But the exterior string-course seen from the staircase itself is an argument equally cogent against the theory. Moreover the mouldings of the arch present a peculiarity which connects it with the date of the chapel rather than with that of the earlier choir. Its mouldings, like those of the pointed arches of entrance to the chapel, are separated by a round hollow instead of the square hollow which appears in the arches of the choir arcade. The doorway must have been inserted very soon after the wall

---

* This would account for the peculiar position of the bases, which do not rest upon the floor of the transept, but are placed considerably above it; like the bases in the choir-aisle, under which there are two steps.

was built, perhaps before the choir was completed. In the cloister doorway, just beyond, the string-course is not similarly treated; but the adoption here of quite a different style of aerchitecture, although its date is very little later, would account for the string-course not being carried over again in this case.

To return to the chapel, it seems the work of the building was interrupted before any floor had been laid down, but the piscinas and aumbries are sufficient evidence that a substantial floor of some kind was laid down not long afterwards. The chapel cannot have been originally built as a chantry chapel, for in this case the founders of the chantries would have supplied the funds for its immediate completion. The piscinas afford a clue to the level of the floor, for they were seldom built at greater height in the wall than 3 ft., and generally lower still. Here they are more than 4 ft. above the bottom of the lower bases. The floor must have covered all the bases as well as the sill of the narrow doorway, the edges of which are at present so clean that it cannot have been used much, if at all. It may be that the floor removed in '25 was the original one. This was 9 in. above the sill and $2\frac{1}{2}$ ft. below the piscinas, and was carried through the doorway into the passage. When the passage was cleared out, amongst the rubbish were found a few German tokens,* two horns, some fragments of Decorated work, and a number of glazed decorative tiles. The tiles were found carefully reared up beside the wall. Many of them are inlaid with letters. Perhaps they are the remains of the flooring of the chapel, and if so we have in them a clue to the use which it was meant to serve. It was the Chancellor's business to manage the educational matters in the church. Here then the choristers and younger members of the church would receive their first lessons in reading, which would be illustrated by the letters on the tiles under their feet. It is to be hoped that some day or other the passage will be opened out by the removal of the brick wall, and then many of the questions here mooted will be cleared up.

---

* Similar tokens have been found under the paving in various parts of the church. They are all stamped with an orb-cross within a trefoil, and on the reverse with crowns and *fleur de lis* alternating. The inscriptions vary: this is a sample—HANS. SCHVLTES. ZV. NURENBR —GLICK. KVMPT. VON. GOT. ISTWAR.

It only remains to say that the restoration of the chapel is now complete. It certainly forms one of the most picturesque bits of architecture to be seen anywhere, and I hope that the authorities will find themselves able to abandon their present intention of screening it off by curtains and dividing it into two parts to be used as vestries. Why not build a vestry in the corresponding position in the south transept, and for an entrance into it, pierce the window-arch which is inserted in the walling up of the large Norman arch.

𝕿𝖍𝖊 𝕮𝖑𝖔𝖎𝖘𝖙𝖊𝖗 𝖆𝖓𝖉 𝕮𝖍𝖆𝖕𝖙𝖊𝖗-𝖍𝖔𝖚𝖘𝖊.

The change from the Early English to the Decorated style of architecture is so very gradual that it is impossible to say when the one ends and the other begins. It is equally difficult to make a definite period to transition. Some of our churches which date back as far the fourth decade of the 13th century shew signs of the triangular, circular, and other geometrical forms of tracery in their windows which have given the name of Geometrical to the style which is generally represented as having prevailed during the reign of the 1st Edward. On the other hand many of the arch-mouldings of the Edwardian period are precisely identical with those belonging to the strictly Early English era. In fact it was not until after the commencement of the 14th century that Decorated architecture began to assume in all its forms a difference sufficient to warrant its being looked upon as a distinct style.

Southwell Minster, with its advanced Early English choir and north transept chapel, the cloisters and chapter-house, four distinctly separate works begun and finished within about seventy years, is an excellent example of this gradual progress of architectural art. Had the north transept chapel its original windows, shewing, probably, how the plain lancet was first divided by mullions to form a triple-lancet window, the example would be almost complete. There is, indeed, an instance of a window of this character of somewhat later date over the cloister doorway in the choir-aisle. But this window is an insertion; its jambs are the jambs of the two lancets which were removed to make way for it, and its arch is made up of the remains of the arches of these lancets. The horizontal rib in the vaulting above it shews a late form of the dog-tooth. The doorway below is fine, and should be noticed before passing through it towards the chapter-house, where the study of one still more beautiful might cause it to be passed by afterwards unobserved. It is a double one. The main arch has two orders: the upper one springs from detached shafts of Purbeck marble; the lower one, a band of foliage over a hollow, rises from the jambs without impost—a feature common in Decorated doorways; the hood terminates on two heads, one crowned and the other mitred. A central shaft, of Purbeck again, carries the two plain subordinate arches; in the spandrel is an open trefoil, and under this a head supporting a bracket for a statue which is lost. The bolts of the door shoot in a curious way into one of the folds of a grotesque serpent crawling up the central shaft.

The Cloister.

The passage leading to the chapter-house is not all of one date. The cloister, that part of it which has the low wooden ceiling, must have been built before the chapter-house, and before the vestibule, which following immediately to connect the two works. We shall consider them, therefore, in this order. The wall arcades of lancet arches are of decidedly early character, and many of the bases, which rest on the stone benches, have the Early English hollow moulding. The capitals, however, are beautifully carved with natural foliage, which in the Decorated style takes the place of the conventional foliage of the preceding style. The west wall with its arcade, the arches of which are trefoiled by cusping, is broken by the external buttresses of the north transept chapel. The arcade on the east side was originally an open one, looking on to a court which is enclosed on the other sides by the chapter-house and the choir-aisle and transept walls. It was evidently blocked up to keep out the cold air, and the extra strength of the walling helps to support the late wall above, which was added to carry the wooden ceiling and pierced with square-headed windows of debased character, in ill accord with the old work. Notwithstanding the fact that a slanting weather-course on the south wall of the vestibule exterior may be seen from the court, I am inclined to think that the cloister was originally quite open without any roof at all, for the wall above the arcade on the west side is not original either. It is altogether different in construction from the wall which carries it, being built of the local stone and merely faced with ash-laring.* To return to the eastern side, if the lower walling were removed a beautiful double arcade of unique design would be displayed. It is carried by two rows of shafts, the space between them measuring 11 inches. Each row carries its series of arches, forming two corresponding arcades, one on the interior face of the walling which blocks this intervening space, the other on the exterior face, and now seen only from the court above-mentioned. Each interior shaft is connected both at base and capital with the corresponding exterior shaft by cross-pins. The cross-pins which connect the capitals are carved on each face with foliage, and from them in each bay springs a broad arch which likewise connects the arches of the

---

* The two upper walls may be of different dates. The western one would be the earlier, being built to carry the slanting roof; and on the removal of this the eastern one with the Perpendicular lights would be added to carry the present roof.

two arcades. They may be seen throughout, for the inserted walling does not rise above the necking of the capitals, the heads of the exterior arches being filled with glazing. The soffits of these internal arches are all plain, excepting that of the arch in the southernmost bay, which is carved with a diaper pattern. This bay forms a means of entrance into the court beyond, and the shafts on the left side have been cut away to make the opening wider. The exterior arcade had suffered much from exposure, and the shafts and bases have recently been renewed. It is to be hoped that some day the whole will be restored to its original form by the removal of the inserted walling. Passing to the north-east corner of the court a pretty view of the tower may be obtained, as well as of other parts of the building which cannot be seen from elsewhere. In the court, besides an ancient stone coffin, there is a discarded stone which is interesting, because it shews how the Early English builders made use of the materials of the Norman choir. It has a string cut on it which may be compared with the string-course separating the second and third stages of the buttresses. On its being turned over the Norman mouldings will be seen. There is a tradition—but only a tradition*—that this court was anciently used as a baptistery; and the fact that a well exists here, though now covered up, gives some colour to the statement. It may receive additional support from its having at one time been reached direct from the choir-aisle by a doorway now blocked up, but its position is plainly marked both on the inside and on the outside. It opened direct towards the spot where the well is, some six or eight feet from it. Moreover it seems to have had a porch or shed over it. A series of dog-tooth, of late character, marks the position of the arch on the outside,

---

* Dickenson, p. 79.

and on the inside its voussoirs of joggled masonry are to be
seen.*

The Chapter-house: Interior.

"What either Cologne Cathedral or Ratisbon or Wiesen
"Kirche are to Germany, Amiens Cathedral or The Sainte
"Chapelle are to France, the Scalegere in Verona to Italy,
"are the Choir of Westminster and the Chapter-house at
"Southwell to England." So writes Mr. G. E. Street, and
assuredly Southwell Chapter-house is placed in the foremost
rank of our Geometrical buildings. In the refined and natural
treatment of the foliage which adorns it, it anticipated the
artistic perfection of works of many years later date, and it
is excelled by none. In its more general features it may be
compared with the earlier parts of the cloisters at Norwich,
and with the ruins of the banqueting-hall in the Palace
grounds at Wells. It strongly reminds one, too, of its con-
temporary, the chapter-house at Wells: in its octagonal shape
it follows the plan adopted in almost all the chapter-houses of
secular communities. The resemblance to York is still more ·
complete, the date of which is uncertain, but it is the only
chapter-house besides Southwell which has no central pillar
to support the vault, and the arrangement is more striking
there on account of its greater size. The diameter of the
Southwell building is only 32½ ft., while in the case of York
it is 57 ft. To confine our attention to Southwell, the vault
is divided into eight cellular compartments, up into which
rise the heads of the large windows which fill the bays. The

* How long this doorway has been blocked up I cannot say, but
in a plan taken in 1797, and extant in the Kerrich collection in the
Brit. Mus. (Add. MSS. 6751) it is shewn, while the doorway in the
cloister arcade is omitted. The latter might easily have been overlooked by the draughtsman, more especially if the former was not
blocked until after that date.

Choir, FROM 1881.

Church-porch.

PLATE IV.

groin-ribs meet in a large boss of foliage in the crown of the
vault. Two wall-ribs rise to form an arch over each window,
and from the apex of this arch a horizontal rib runs along the
crown of each cellular compartment to the central boss. Two
additional pairs of ribs rise up the sides of the compartment
meeting in the horizontal rib. All the ribs shew deep hollow
mouldings almost Early English in character, and at every
intersection there is a boss of foliage. The window arches
consist of two orders in each, springing from engaged jamb-
shafts. Each window is divided into three cusped lancet lights
of equal heights, and the head is filled in with three cusped
circles, the central and highest being quatrefoiled, the remaining two trefoiled. Above the head of the middle light rises
a sharper pointed arch, which touches the uppermost circle,
and incloses an irregular cusped space. Under the window is
a sloping sill, on which the jamb-shafts rest. And under the
sills again runs a string-course, separating the stages and
consisting of the Decorated scroll-moulding above a deep
undercut hollow separated from it by a fillet. The capitals
of the vaulting shafts, which rise up the angles of the building
from the stone bench all round the walls, are on a level with
the capitals of the jamb-shafts of the windows. All the
capitals are enriched with foliage, and the foliage forms a
continuous band which serves to connect each vaulting-shaft
with the jamb-shafts on each side of it, so that together they
appear to form a single shafted pillar. All these shafts are
keeled—to adopt Mr. Dimock's term—like those in the north
transept chapel.

The space between the bench and the window sills is
occupied by a range of stalls, which form an arcade running
round the building, five in each side or bay. The arcade
merits the most minute examination. The arches are
foiled (that is to say their entire suite of mouldings follows

their trefoiled form) and their mouldings are deeply shaded
with filleted rounds and hollows. They spring from single
circular detached shafts, the capitals of which are beautifully
enriched with deeply undercut foliage, in almost every case
copied from nature. The one or two exceptions remind us of
the conventional triple-leafed foliage of the Early English
style. The bases, too, which rest upon the stone bench, in
the form and variety of their mouldings remind us of the
base-mouldings of the choir piers. The triple roll-moulding
is the more common form, but in some cases we still find the
hollow replacing the middle roll. Conforming to the characteristic of the later style the lower roll overhangs the plinth,
and the latter is octagonal. In the bases of the jamb-shafts
of the windows above the change of style is more clearly
marked: here the mouldings consist of two small rounds
above a much larger overhanging one. To return to the
arcade. Above each arch an acute gablet forms a canopy over
it. The gablets form a continuous series, broken only by the
vaulting-shafts in the angles. They spring from corbels—
heads, bosses of foliage, or grotesque animals—placed between
the arches, and rise through the string-course to terminate
in finials. Most of the finials are restorations in composition.
A series of crockets—no longer of the early form like the
bishop's crook which we noticed in the exterior—adorn the
straight sides of the gablets. There are two distinct forms,
one apparently representing oak leaves; but all the crockets
are regular and formal when compared with the rest of the
carving, and they stand well clear of the wall, allowing their
shadow to be seen upon it behind them. The two lower ones
above each corbel are made to overlap in an effective way.
The triangular spandrel-space between the apex of each arch
and the canopy above it is sculptured with natural foliage,
vying with the capitals in variety of design and delicacy of

treatment. In a few cases it is made to grow, as it were, out of the open mouth of a head or some grotesque figure placed in the centre of the spandrel. The foliage of the capitals stands away apparently quite free of their bell-mouldings, and if a finger be placed on the inner side of the leaves they will be found to have been finished off quite smooth. The stems running behind the foliage will be found to be quite perfect though they cannot be seen except in one or two places where the leaves have unfortunately been broken away. In one instance there is an animal hidden away behind the leaves, and it can only be seen by looking up from underneath the capital. Over each capital a spray of oak, vine, or some other plant, covers the mitring of the arch-mouldings.

Mr. Dimock has so well described the general beauties of the carving that I cannot do better than quote his words. "The "foliage everywhere is most beautiful: the oak, the vine, the "hop, the ivy, the maple, the white-thorn, the rose, with a "vast variety of other plants, are sculptured with exquisite "freedom and delicacy; and no two capitals or bosses or "spandrels can be found alike, no wearisome repetition of "beautiful parts tires the eye, but everywhere we meet, in "ever-changing and ever-charming variety, with some fresh "object of interest and admiration. What is very usual in "work of this date, figures are frequently introduced amidst "the foliage: I have already mentioned the heads, with "branches issuing from the mouth, which occur in the span- "drels above the stalls: others of the spandrels have birds or "lizard-like monsters: in the capitals, a man reclines beneath "a tree, puffing lustily away at a horn, or a goat is gnawing "the leaves, or a bird pecking the berries, or a pair of pigs "are grunting up the acorns, or a brace of hounds just grab- "bing a hare. Unhappily there has been much injury, from " wet finding its way through broken windows and defective

"roof, and very much from wanton mutilation; still, no more
"beautiful and interesting sculpture perhaps is to be found in
"any church in England. Of very much of it it is not too
"much to say, that it is the work of no mere chiseller of
"stone, but of a consummate artist; than whom it may be
"well doubted whether any sculptor, of any age or country,
"ever produced anything more life-like and exquisitely
"graceful." A newel staircase, leading to the roof and to a
small room over the vestibule, abuts upon the south-west side
of the octagon, which, therefore, has no window in it. The
wall on this side shews a blank arch with tracery and mullions
in imitation of the windows, but it is not quite so high as
they are, and the space above it is relieved by sculptured
foliage. A similar arrangement is seen over the doorway in
the west side. The doorway is not built in the centre of this
side, but further south, in the centre of the vestibule. A
portable parclose or screen must at one time have fitted into
the doorway on the interior.

As seen from the vestibule this doorway is a very beautiful
one. It is a double one, the arch being divided by a slender
clustered shaft in the centre, which carries two subordinate
trefoiled arches, with a quatrefoiled circle above them. The
mouldings consist of filleted rounds separated by a filleted
hollow. In the subordinate arches the hollow is enriched by
a leaf ornament arranged quite regularly, just as a ball-flower
might have been. The ball-flower, which became so common
later on in the style, and is found even in buildings of the
same date, taking the place of the Early English dog-tooth,
is not used in the chapter-house. The cusps of the arches and
the circle above them is a continuation of the filleted round
which forms their inner moulding. They are all pierced.
The capital of the central shaft is enriched with foliage, but
the corresponding jamb-shafts have no capitals, the abacus

only of the adjoining capitals being continued round them.
Above their innermost order, which contains the doorway
proper, the arch consists of three orders of voussoirs, and the
whole is surmounted by a hood-mould so closely connected
that it has the appearance of an additional order. The middle
order of the three is a broad circular band of foliage consisting
of two strings of leaves worked upon two hollows, separated
by a keeled round. The foliage stands quite free of the
hollows, attached only to their edges, and a close examination
will shew that the hollows themselves are as cleanly chiselled
as any of the more exposed mouldings. The masonry here is
very fine, and the joints of the stems of the foliage worked
upon the different voussoirs is wonderfully accurate. The
orders on each side of this one are separated from it by hollows,
and themselves moulded with rounds and hollows, some of
the rounds being filleted some scrolled. All three spring from
detached circular shafts of Purbeck, a decidedly Early English
feature. In the jamb of the arch, between the shafts, there
are small mouldings, one a plain round, the other filleted.
The three bases are more Decorated in character; two small
rounds above a larger one overlapping the octagonal part,
which is divided into two parts by somewhat similar mouldings which encircle the bases and run across the jamb in the
form of a string. The rich capitals are like those we have
already examined inside the chapter-house. The three capitals
are carved on one large stone, and their deep-cut foliage being
carved continuously unites them across the jamb. The hood-
mould comprises a plain round moulding and another equally
beautiful band of foliage worked upon a deep-cut hollow. It
springs from detached shafts with bases and capitals like those
just described, and placed, not in the jamb, but apart in the
plane of the wall, a portion of which intervenes between
them and the adjoining jamb. On the edge of the wall is

worked a small round moulding, which runs up without any impost round the arch, combining itself with the mouldings of the superior order. Between this round and the adjoining jamb-shaft there is a hollow moulding, up which a band of foliage runs, connecting itself with the foliage of the capital. The shafts from which the hood-mould springs also carry two small acute arches on the face of the wall, one on each side of the archway.

The Vestibule shews in its design an attempt to assimilate the details of the two buildings which it connects. In the arcading, forsaking the foiled form of the chapter house arches, it returns to the cusped form of those in the cloister arcade, and the crocketed gablets of the former give way to the continuous hood-mould of the latter. The bases retain the later form used in the doorway, which differs from that used either in the cloister or chapter-house interior.

The windows above are much plainer than those of the chapter-house. There is one order less in the arches; the three lancet lights have no cusps, and the additional acute arch over the middle one is absent. The capitals, however, are equally beautiful, and being lower, can more easily be examined. The vaulting is quadripartite, and the shafts are filleted instead of keeled. The shafts which carry the low arch communicating with the cloister rise up each side into the mouth of a head, on which the capital rests. On the west side the buttress of the north transept chapel divides the two works. The junction on the other side is in the middle of one of the arches of the arcade some feet further south. The half-arch of the cloister arcade has been altered to suit the higher pitch of the later work. The cloister string-course above the arcade ends in a grotesque head gnawing a bunch of foliage. The vestibule string-course ends in the figure of a man, and the half-arch rises into the back of a monster which he is bestriding. The device is curious and ingenious.

The Organ Screen.

The stone screen between the piers of the eastern tower-arch, which now carries the organ, must once have carried the great rood. It is pure Decorated work so profusely enriched with ornament that, in describing it, it is impossible to do more than notice the leading features of its design. It opens into the nave with three canopied arches having pierced foliations. The remarkable stone roof has the appearance of a sham vault. It is flat, has a longitudinal rib, and is supported by flying ribs. Above each flying rib there is a horizontal rib on the actual roof, and in the open spandrel between them there is a trefoiled circle. The three arches and the flying ribs spring from slender pillars of four clustered shafts. The base-mouldings shew the characteristic feature of the lower round considerably overlapping the octagonal plinth. The close-clinging foliage of the capitals also is characteristic of the style, contrasting with the freely carved and more natural foliage of the early Decorated capitals of the chapter-house. The side walls are richly panelled with flowing tracery above a canopied and foliated arch. Passing through the doorway under the inner central arch we stand between the staircases leading to the gallery above and under another vault, the ribs of which afford a curious example of interpretation.

On the choir side there are three prebendal *miserere** stalls on each side of the central archway. The central ogee-arch is cinquefoiled and crocketed, and, rising under a sharply-

---

* On the subsellia of the stalls are carvings, chiefly of stiff-leaved foliage called misereres. The seats are fixed with hinges, and when they are turned up the miserere forms a kind of bracket of sufficient projection to afford considerable rest to anyone leaning upon it. They were of old used by ecclesiastics when they had to perform long services or penitentials standing. Miserere stalls are very common, and

H

pointed label forming a gablet, enriched with crockets and a band of foliage, supports a figure of the Virgin seated and nursing the Child. In the spandrels above the gablet are two small trefoiled canopies over figures of angels which stand on rich corbels of foliage and face towards the central figure of the Virgin. The mouldings of the arch below consist of a hollow between filleted rounds, under which is a band of foliage; the cusps terminate in heads, and the spandrels formed by them are adorned with foliage. Over each of the stalls is a similarly cinquefoiled arch, crocketed and finialed, the crockets being of a square shape and set so close together as to form in appearance a continuous band of foliage. The shafts which divide the stalls and support the arches rise between them to support at some distance above a series of gablets, and, rising between these, again terminate in small pinnacles. The gablets, crocketed and finialed and enriched with the characteristic ball-flower, have the appearance of triangular-headed arches above the stall canopies. The wall-face within them is panelled with mullions and beautiful flowing tracery, which over the middle stall on each side is pierced, opening through the arches which support the roof of the screen into the nave beyond. The whole is surmounted by a parapet, its tracery running along in a continuous undulation, pierced and foliated. The curious figures from which the gablets spring should be noticed. The gablet over the central arch springs on the one side from a head in a chain-mail hood, on the other from a crowned head. The

afford representations of grotesque animals, of scriptural subjects often irreverently treated, of scenes from domestic life, and of stories from the mediæval romances. Boston Church has as many as 64 stalls, and their misereres have been fully described by the Bishop Suffragan of Nottingham, the Right Rev. E. Trollope, in Vol X. of *Ass. Arch. Societies' Reports and Papers*, 1870.—See Mr. M. H. Bloxam's *Internal Arrangement of Churches* in Vol. II. of *Gothic Architecture*, invaluable to the student.

back of the first stall on the south side of the entrance is ornamented with carved diaper-work, in which there is no fixed pattern, each square shewing a different flower from its fellows. In later times this was the seat of the Vicar-General.

The position of the responds of the choir arcade in close proximity to the Norman piers, and the small Early English arch between them on the south side leading to the stairs to the organ·loft, suggested to Mr. Dimock the view that a rood-screen, coeval with the choir, was removed to make way for the present one. This view has been confirmed on the removal of the side stalls, whereby the inner part of the base of the Early English respond has been partially exposed. The bases of the shafts on this side have no mouldings like those on the aisle side, but are simply chamfered, proving that they were not seen in the original arrangement. This screen, too, must have been a wooden one.

It is unlikely that any screen stood here in the Norman church, the choir of which extended, possibly, into the·space under the lantern tower. There may have been a screen, however, between the piers of the western tower-arch.

The Sedilia.

The sedilia are Decorated work, similar in many points to the rood-screen, but somewhat later in date. They are five in number. Quintuple sedilia are very rare. Three is the usual number of seats, to which the priest officiating at high mass retired with his attendant ministers, the deacon and sub-deacon, during the chanting of the *Gloria in excelsis*.* Quad-ruple sedilia are found at Gloucester Cathedral. Here they are crowned with ogee-arched canopies, ornamented with double foliations, crockets, and finials. The crockets are

* Mr. H. M. Bloxam's *Gothic Architecture.*

116

singularly beautiful : each one has its middle part raised and
its edges attached to the sides of the arch, and under it an
additional spray of natural foliage turning over towards the
crocket below. Groups of figures rest between the canopies,
forming a peculiar feature in the general design.* What the
groups are intended to represent it is in some cases difficult to
determine. The easternmost figure doubtless represents the
Almighty supporting the globe, symbolic of the creation, and
the next group of two figures is thought by some to be intended
for the second and third Persons of the Trinity. The westernmost group evidently pourtrays the flight into Egypt, while
the two next groups also may relate to the Virgin Mary, to
whom the church is dedicated. East of the sedilia is a piscina
under a low canopied arch.†

The fire of 1711 destroyed both organ and bells. The organ
was rebuilt by a German named Smith, and the bells replaced

---

* All the heads of the figures, together with the finials and much
of the ornamental details of the sedilia, are restorations in Roman
cement.

† The following passage is quoted from Clarke and Killpack's
History and Antiquities of the Church, published by Mr. Whittingham
in '39 :—" The situation of the sedilia was formerly occupied by an
" oak screen. The singing-boys used to amuse themselves by climbing
" to the top of the screen until a fatal accident happened to one of
" their number by its falling down upon him, which occasioned its
" removal, and the building of the wall in which the sedilia is inserted
" in its place ; its sculptured ornaments and figures were taken from
" various parts of the interior upon making alterations therein."
There cannot be the slightest doubt, however, that the sedilia are
original Decorated work. Mr. Killpack's mistake arose doubtless
from the fact that the sedilia in those days were in a very dilapidated
condition, and they were, on the removal of the screen after this
accident to Thomas Bucklow, "a fine boy of nine years of age,"
restored, I believe by the same artist, Bernasconi, who similarly
repaired the rood screen and built the side stalls. The minor matter
of the removal of the screen, which had evidently been placed there
to hide the dilapidations of the sedilia, is mentioned in the chapter
records, but they are silent about the more important "insertion of
the sedilia."

by Ruddall of Gloucester. Three out of the eight have been re-cast, or new bells hung in their stead :—

1st. Abr Ruddall of Gloucester cast us all 1721.
2nd. G Mears founders London 1849.
3rd. Prosperity to this Town.
4th. T Mears of London fecit 1819.
5th. T Mears of London fecit 1819.
6th. Prosperity to the Chapter.
7th. Prosperity to the Church of England.
8th. I to the Church the Living call
And to the Grave do summon all.

In the original peal the 2nd, 4th, and 5th bells bore the following inscriptions :—

2nd. Peace and Good Neighbourhood.
4th. Prosperity to our Benefactors.
5th. From Lightning and Tempest Good Lord Deliver us.

The chimes are set to the National Anthem.

Measurements.

Length (Internal)	306 Feet.
Breadth	60¼ ,,
Length of Great Transept	123 ,,
Height of Lantern Tower	105 ,,
Height of Western Towers	99 ,,
Height of Spires	50 ,,

Proportions of Norman Church.

UNIT = C. 30 FEET.

Total Length	8
Total Breadth	4
Breadth of Nave and Choir (with Aisles) ..	2
Breadth of Chancel and Transepts	9/10
Length of Nave	5
Length of Choir	2
Length of each Transept	1

CHAPTER V.

EFFIGIES AND SEPULCHRAL SLABS—SCULPTURE—GLAZING.

Effigies and Sepulchral Slabs.

Southwell Minster is not rich, numerically speaking, in
effigies. It contains only two in fact, but the famous effigy
of Archbishop Sandys is one of them. Nor is there a single
monumental brass of any size left to tell its tale. Of the few
brassless slabs that remain, one is interesting. It lies in the
north transept, and shews the figures of a knight and his
lady—the knight in armour, with a helmet on his head, sword
and dagger by his side, a lion at his feet, and a shield in each
corner of the slab.

In the north nave-aisle there is a goodly number of sepulchral slabs with crosses incised. They have been squared and
laid down with the new paving. The remnant of an altar
slab, shewing three out of the five crosses, has unfortunately
suffered the same fate. Many of the crosses are good examples of the beautiful incised crosses of the 13th and 14th
centuries. That in the second bay dates probably as early as
the reign of Richard I. or of John. A cross flory in the first
bay, and two very similar ones lying under the step inside the
cloister doorway, probably belong to the first half of the 13th
century. There are many crosses of somewhat later date
perhaps—that, for instance, incised on a slab also in the
second bay, which shews, too, a chalice, indicating that it
covered the body of a priest.* The chalice is tipped just as
the priest would tip it in Celebration. Two of the crosses
are decidedly early date, probably the 12th century. One of
them, lying in the first bay, is sketched in Plate III. (No. 9).
No. 10 in the same plate is the remnant of a slab which was

---

* See sketch No. 8 in Plate III.

recently found under the flooring under the lantern tower, shewing a cross of somewhat similar character. No: 11 is another remnant lately found—the incised figure of an ecclesiastic probably. In the first bay lies the incised figure of a female, I believe, with the hands joined in a devotional attitude. In the second bay, under a sepulchral recess in the wall, there is an altar tomb, upon which has been placed a slab with a beautiful raised cross upon it.

In the floor on the opposite side of the nave is an inscribed stone which has been most ingeniously restored. It was found in the flooring of the south transept cut in two and squared, and robbed thereby of two or three letters in the middle of each line of the inscription. In laying it down in its present position a blank space has been left for these letters. The inscription when restored reads thus :—

GVILIELMV	S FIL	IVS GVIL
IELMI THO	RNTO	N ET MIL
LICENTIÆ	EIVS	VXORIS PRO
BÆ INDOLI	S ET I	NGENII PVER
ET HVIVS E	CCLE	SIÆ CHO
RISTA ANN	VM A	GENS
SVÆ ÆTAT	IS DE	CIMVM
QVARTV	M	DISCES
SIT PRIMO		

In a sepulchral recess in the secondary transept on the south side of the choir lies a much mutilated effigy of a priest. Mr. Bloxam describes it as of alabaster, in high relief, representing the party commemorated as vested in the amice, alb with parures, stole, and chasuble, with the maniple over the left arm. The head and hands are gone. The same authority, judging from the material, thinks it to be of the 15th century. It is not in its original position. Gough describes it as lying on the north side of the church, partly in it, partly in a chapel of the north aisle, on an altar tomb adorned with five blank shields, quaterfoils, on each of the two sides, "under a "canopy of tabernacle work, fragments of which lie behind "with a whole length figure of an angel." All this has disappeared, but the canopy, as shewn in one of Dickenson's plates, confirms Mr. Bloxam's opinion that the effigy belongs to the 15th century. The *amice* is the garment thrown round the shoulders. The *alb*, a closely-fitting tunic reaching to the feet, was so called because it was made of white linen. The *maniple* was given, in the 11th century, to sub-deacons as the badge of their order, and its original use, therefore, seems to have been to clean therewith the sacred vessels.* The *chasuble* was the priest's principal vestment, and always worn in the Celebration of the Mass. Its early form was that of a complete circle, with an opening in the centre for the head to go through. Mr. Bloxam tells us the Roman *pænula*, or travelling cloak, was the prototype of this vestment.

On the death of Edward VI. Dr. Edwin Sandys, then Vice-Chancellor of Cambridge University, was commanded by Northumberland to preach a sermon in support of Lady Jane Grey's claim to the crown, in consequence of which he was imprisoned by Queen Mary. On his release soon after he proceeded to join the exiles in Germany, and took part in "the Troubles at Frankfort" (1544). At this time, be it noted, he expressed his willingness to dispense with the use of the surplice in public worship. Returning home on the accession of Queen Elizabeth, he was consecrated Bishop of Winchester. Translated to London in 1570, he became Archbishop of York in 1577, and filled the see till his death in 1588. His effigy now stands in the north transept, its second or third resting place since its removal from its original position in the chancel on the north side of the altar-table. It is a recumbent figure in alabaster; the head and feet rest on cushions supported by angels, one at each corner of the tomb. In the front of the tomb are represented his widow and nine children—seven sons and two daughters—kneeling; at one end are the arms of Sandys, at the other a lengthy Latin inscription describing his character, life, and sufferings. The effigy is chiefly interesting for the bearing it has upon the Elizabethan disputes about ecclesiastical vestments. The archbishop is represented† as vested in the chasuble or *vestment*, which, unlike the chasubles seen in effigies of early date, is very long behind, and is folded back under the figure, reaching from the feet nearly to the shoulders: this is edged with lace and worn over the rochet and chimere; the tippet

---

* Hook's *Church Dictionary.*   † See No. 16, Plate III.

or almuce falls over the shoulders and in front of the breast in folds; and the hood fastened beneath the chin and thrown back behind.

With regard to the unusual form of the chasuble, it appears that in late pre-Reformation times it had become somewhat fashionable to wear the vestment longer behind than in front. There is no effigy or monumental brass which shews so peculiarly long a vestment as the one here, but there are not a few brasses, I believe, which illustrate the prevailing fashion in a less degree. Bishop Veasey, of Exeter, whose effigy lies in Sutton Coldfield Church, Warwickshire, is represented in a vestment reaching nearly to the feet. He died in 1554, but Mr. Bloxam thinks the effigy was executed some years before his death. The chimere of black silk and the white rochet formed the usual episcopal dress from the reign of Elizabeth onwards. They were often accompanied by the academical hood and square cap, but in this effigy the head is a restoration, so that the latter (if it ever was there) does not appear. The hands are also a restoration: but, according to the engraving in Drake's *Eboracum*, they originally held a book instead of being joined in prayer. The tippet is a merely canonical habit.

Let us briefly review the historical position. The Rubric of the first Prayer Book (1549) of Edward VI. enjoined the following eucharistic vestments for a bishop—his rochet, an albe *or* surplice, and a vestment *or* cope; for a priest—a plain white albe, with a vestment *or* cope. Up to this date the vestment or chasuble (for the terms, be it noted, are synonymous, the chasuble being the vestment *par excellence*) had been considered a necessary part of the officiating priest's dress, while the cope was merely a processional habit. The Rubric placed these distinctive habits on the same footing, and from henceforth the cope might be used at the Celebration instead of the chasuble, and the surplice instead of the albe. In Edward VI's. second Prayer Book (1552) the Rubric was altered thus: "The minister, in "time of Communion, shall use neither alb, vestment, nor cope; but "being an archbishop or bishop he shall have and wear a rochet, and "being a priest or deacon he shall have and wear a surplice only." In the first year of Queen Elizabeth an Act of Uniformity was passed re-establishing the second Prayer Book of Edward VI., but a special provision was made "that such Ornaments of the Church and "of the Ministers thereof shall be retained and used as was in the "Church of England by the authority of Parliament, in the second "year of the reign of Edward the Sixth, until other order shall be "therein taken by the Authority of the Queen's Majesty, with the "advice of her Commissioners appointed and authorized under the "Great Seal of England for causes Ecclesiastical, or of the metro- "politan of this Realm."

In the Injunctions of Elizabeth, issued in 1559, the one dealing with the Apparel of Ministers runs as follows:—"Item. Her Majesty "being desirous to have the Prelacy and Clergy of this Realm to be "held as well in outward reverence, as otherwise regarded for the "worthiness of their ministries, and thinking it necessary to have "them known to the people in all places and assemblies both in the "Church and without, and thereby to receive the honour and estima- "tion due to the special messengers and ministers of Almighty God; "willeth and commandeth that all Archbishops and Bishops, and all "other that be called or admitted to preaching or ministry of the "Sacraments, or that be admitted into vocation ecclesiastical, or into "any Society of Learning in either of the Universities, or elsewhere, "shall use and wear such seemly habits, garments, and such square "caps as were most commonly and orderly received in the later year "of the reign of King Edward the Sixth, not thereby meaning to "attribute any holiness or special worthiness to the said garments, "but as S. Paul writeth, *omnia decenter et secundum ordinem fiant,*"

Whether the Injunctions had or had not the force of an Act of Parliament I do not stop to inquire. In either case the *legality* of the use of the vestments enjoined by Edward VI's. first Prayer Book was not affected by them, for they undoubtedly refer, not to the vestments to be worn by the clergy in public worship, but only to their secular and academical habit. That this is so is proved by the evidence we have of the subsequent use of other vestments than the episcopal rochet and the priest's surplice, which, and which only, would have been legal if the Injunction were intended to bring about a return to the vestments commanded to be used in public worship in the later year of Edward VI. The consecration of Matthew Parker as Abp. of Canterbury took place in 1559, only a few months after the issue of the Injunction. Parker entered the chapel in his academical habit; he wore a surplice during the performance of the Rite, and immedi- ately afterwards laid it aside and assumed the episcopal rochet and chimere together with the canonical almuce or tippet. Barlow and Soory, Bishops of Chichester and Hereford, were also vested in rochet and chimere. During the Rite of Consecration Barlow wore a silken cope. Again, in the Convocation of 1562, the following motion was proposed: "That the use of vestments, copes, and surplices be from "henceforth taken away." If the cope was legal, then must the chasuble or vestment have been legal also. There can be no doubt that the cope was often worn, but only in cathedrals and collegiate churches, and seldom in parish churches. And it is equally clear that the vestment, though legal, was seldom if ever worn after the date of Edward VI's. first Prayer Book. The Rubric enjoined the use of one of the two, and permitted the use of either, with the result that "the vestiment is put away and the coape retayned," and likewise "the albe is layed aside and the surplesse is used." The vestments were actually sold, *or* "defaced and made into a clothe for the pulpit "and coion table." The very name fell into disuse, and in 1570 we find the Latin *casula* translated into the English *cope*. The presence of the chasuble in the effigy of Sandys is in itself sufficient proof of its legality in the reign of Elizabeth.

Abp. Sandys shewed himself a strong Reformer throughout.

During "the Troubles at Frankfort" he even went so far as to declare himself willing to dispense with the surplice. While the bill which resulted in the Act of Uniformity of 1668 was in progress, Sandys wrote to Parker thus: "The last book of service [1562] is gone "through, with a proviso to retain the ornaments which were used "in the first and second years of King Edward, until it please the "Queen to take other order for them. Our gloss upon this text is, "that we shall not be forced to use them, but that others in the "meantime shall not convey them away, but that they may remain "for the Queen." Two years later he wrote to Peter Martyr: "Tantum manent in ecclesia nostra vestimenta illa papistica, capas "intellige, quas diu non duraturus speramus;" and he doubtless did all he could to abolish the use of the cope throughout his diocese and province. His inclinations, then, being so strongly averse to the ancient episcopal vestments, how is it that his effigy is apparelled in the chasuble? The peculiar form of the vestment, together with its combination with the episcopal rochet and chimere and with the academical hood, a combination which has no parallel instance, has been considered a proof that the effigy is no conventional representation of a Bishop on the part of the artist, and that the Archbishop actually wore the chasuble during his lifetime.* But it is difficult to believe that he would uphold a practice so utterly at variance with his declared views. Mr. Bloxam, an eminent authority on ecclesiastical vestments, writes :† "Perhaps the subsequent proceedings of "the ultra-Puritan Reformers against the discipline of the Church of "England, of which the attack upon the vestments was but a part, "and of which, as prelate, he might foresee the results, occasioned "this, his silent protest after death, against the extreme opinions of "his party. Who knows? I can but hazard a conjecture."‡ There is a tradition that Abp. Sandys' son was a man of more conservative

---

* Mr. J. T. Micklethwaite thinks that the Abp. must have worn "this queer long-tailed chasuble, though it may be that he called it "a cope." But Sandys shewed himself equally averse to the cope.

† *Ass. Arch. Societies'* Vol. for 1859. I have not had any opportunity of doing more than cursorily examining the paper, but I have here to acknowledge the large use I have made throughout this notice of Mr. Bloxam's valuable chapter on *The Vestments prescribed by the Church in and from the reign of Edward VI.* in the *Companion to Gothic Arch.* published by Bell and Son, 1882.

‡ I do not know whether the following extract from the will of Abp. Sandys, dated as early as 1558, may be cited in support of this view or not : "Fourthly, concerning rites and ceremonies by political "institutions authorized among us, as I am and have been persuaded, "that such as are now sett down by publick authority in the Church "of England are in no way either ungodly or unlawfull, but that "may with good conscience for order and obedience sake be used of a "good Christian—for the private baptism to be ministered by women "I neither take to be prescribed or permitted—so have I ever been "and presently am persuaded that some of them be not so expedient "for this church now, but that in the church reformed, and in all this "time of the gospell wherein the seed of the scripture hath so long

views than his father, and that it was he who had this effigy executed by a foreign artist.

It only remains to add that Tideswell Church, Derbyshire, contains an incised brass effigy of Robert Pursglove, representing him in the ancient episcopal vestments: alb, stole, dalmatic, and chasuble; amice with apparel, pastoral staff and mitre. The chasuble is considerably longer behind than in front. Pursglove was Bishop Suffragan of Hull, but preferred to resign his bishopric to taking the Oath of Supremacy in 1559. He died in 1579 This may very possibly be an instance of one who continued to use the vestment long after it had fallen into general disuse.

There is a sepulchral slab lying in the north porch incised with a small tau-cross and a heart with the date 1536. It bears also an inscription, but I have not yet succeeded in making this out. The tau-cross, in form like the Greek letter tau or *t*, is sufficiently significant and uncommon to call for special notice. Mr. Charles Boutell tells us it is the symbol of an order established on the continent and styled the Order of S. Anthony. At Ingham, in Norfolk, there are effigies of Sir Roger de Bois and his Lady, bearing date 1360 and wearing mantles charged with the tau-cross having the word ANTHON in chief.* Hulme Abbey, Northumberland, contained a sepulchral slab incised with a large tau-cross pierced with three nails. At Welbeck Priory, Notts, there is a fragment of a slab with a hand in relief, holding a tau staff, probably the official insignia of the prior.†

"been sown, they may better be disused by little and little than more
"and more urged. Howbeit, as I do easily acknowledge our ecclesi-
"astical policy in some points may be bettered, so I do utterly mislike,
"even in my conscience, all such rude and indigested platforms as
"have been more lately and boldly than either learnedly and wisely
"preferred, tending, not to the reformation, but to the destruction of
"this Church of England—the particularities of both sorts referred
"to the discretion of the godly wise. Of the latter I can only say
"thus, that the state of a small private church, and the forme of a
"larger Christian kingdome, neither would long like, nor can at all
"broke, one and the same ecclesiastical government. This much I
"thought to testify concerning these ecclesiastical matters, to clear
"me from all suspicion of double and indirect dealing in the house of
"God, wherein, as touching mine office, I have not haulted, but
"walked sincerely according to that skill and ability which I have
"received at God's mercifull hands."

* The badge of the Courtenay family, a tau-cross with a bell attached, is sculptured in the Palace at Exeter.—Mr. Chas. Boutell's *English Heraldry.*   † Haines, *Manual of Sepulchral Slabs.*

In connection with the tau-cross we must notice the remarkable slab, now lying loose in the vestibule, but formerly in the flooring of the choir, which has a small incised cross at each corner and the following inscription :

𝕳𝖎𝖈 𝖏𝖆𝖈𝖊𝖙 𝖂𝖎𝖑𝖑'𝖒𝖘 𝕿𝖆𝖑𝖇𝖔𝖙 𝖒𝖎𝖘𝖊𝖗
𝖊𝖙 𝖎𝖓𝖉𝖎𝖌𝖓𝖚𝖘 𝕾𝖆𝖈𝖊𝖗𝖉𝖔𝖘 𝖊𝖝𝖕𝖊𝖈𝖙𝖆𝖓𝖘
𝖗𝖊𝖘𝖚𝖗𝖗𝖊𝖈'𝖎𝖔𝖓𝖊𝖒 𝖒𝖔𝖗𝖙𝖚𝖔𝖗𝖚𝖒 𝖘'𝖇 𝖘𝖎𝖌𝖓𝖔 𝖙𝖍𝖆𝖚.

Here lies William Talbot wretched
and unworthy Priest awaiting
the resurrection of the dead under the sign of the cross.

A writer in the *Archæological Journal*[*] tells us the expression "sub signo thau" thus used has not occurred elsewhere, but that frequent instances have been noticed, in mediæval books of art, of similar allusions to the Thau, regarded, doubtless, as typical of the symbol of salvation. in Ezekiel's vision, ch. ix. verse 4. In the Vulgate the passage runs thus:— Transi per mediam civitatem in medio Jerusalem: et *signa thau* super frontes virorum gementium, et dolentium super cunctis abominationibus, quæ fiunt in medio ejus *:*—Go through the midst of the city, through the midst of Jerusalem, and *mark a cross* upon the fore-heads of the men that sigh and lament over all the abominations which are done in the midst thereof. The expression seems to have been suggested by the Hebrew—*mark a mark*, or as we might now render it, *cross a cross*—where the word used is *tav*, the name of the Hebrew letter *t*. This letter was formed like a cross in the Phœnician alphabet, but not in the Hebrew. In the LXX. it is rendered *dos semeion*, and in the authorised version, *set a mark*, merely.

William Talbot, canon of Southwell, lived in the latter part of the 15th century. He will be mentioned again as having contributed largely to the repairs of the Vicars' College in the year 1484.

Sculpture.

The sculptured stone which now forms the lintel of the belfry doorway in the north transept is very interesting. It must at one time have been the tympanum of an earlier doorway, and a part of it has unfortunately been cut away to make it fit into its present position. The sculpture embodies

---

[*] Vol. XIV. 76.

a double subject, rudely executed in low relief, the one representing probably David rescuing the lamb from the lion, the other very clearly representing S. Michael encountering the dragon. S. Michael forms the central figure, holding in his right hand an uplifted sword, while on his left arm he carries a circular shield with which he is warding off the attack of the dragon. The head and shoulders of the figure supposed to represent David have been cut away. He is kneeling on one knee, and on the other rests one of the fore-feet of the lion. His right hand is in the mouth of the lion, grasping its lower jaw, while with his left hand he seems to be pushing up the animal's upper jaw. The lamb is represented with its fore-feet resting on the lion's head, and its hind-quarters hanging in mid-air. The sculpture cannot be of later date than the middle of the 11th century, when the church seems to have been considerably enlarged, perhaps altogether rebuilt, and it might be of earlier date still.

I have not met with any other instance of a representation, either in sculpture or mural painting, of David and the lion. An Anglo-Saxon MS. of the earlier half of the 11th century contains a drawing apparently of the same subject.* The lamb is absent. David is seen in a very uncomfortable position on the back of the lion, his two hands *in the mouth of the animal* separating its jaws, and the lion's head turned upwards and backwards towards him. The dragon was a favourite animal wherewith the Anglo-Saxons ornamented their books in the borders and initials. The dragon which forms the initial V in the MS. of Cœdmon (10th century), of which also Mr. Wright gives a drawing, bears a resemblance to the dragon in this sculpture. Tne interweaving folds of the tail remind one of the sculpturing seen on the Derbyshire Saxon crosses. But a dragon very similar in design may be seen on a Norman capital in Shobdon Church, Herefordshire, of much later date; in this case the sculpture is much richer and more delicately treated. Mr. Bloxam informs me that on a Norman tympan over a doorway in Hallaton Church, Leicestershire, the subject of S. Michael and the dragon is similarly treated, and that in that case also the shield is circular. The subject, however, is a rare one, and S Michael is more often depicted, especially in mural paintings, with a pair of scales weighing souls.

---

* MS. Cotton., Tiberius CVI. Mr. Wright gives a cut of this drawing in his *History of Caricature and Grotesque in Art*.

Here I may call attention to the marks upon the pier dividing the two easternmost bays of the nave arcade on the south
side.   They merely shew the outline of a life-size sculpture,
either in stone or wood, which once rested against the pier,
representing the Virgin on one side, the angel Gabriel, holding a scroll, on the other, and the Lily, the emblem of purity,
springing up from a pot between the two figures.   A few
moments' study reveals the whole subject very clearly, and it
doubtless indicates that underneath it there stood an altar
dedicated·to the Virgin Mary, the bay being occupied by the
chantry-chapel of "Our Lady."*

No less interesting than the early tympanum just described
are the sculptured capitals of the eastern tower-arch as seen
from the organ-loft.   The responds of this arch consist of
three attached semi-cylindrical shafts, the capitals of which
shew an imitation of the Ionic volute, and on all except one

---

* In treating of the chantry-chapels in an earlier chapter (I. 28) I
find, on carefully comparing lists of different dates, that I have
fallen into some errors. Speaking of the chapels as they existed in
1372 I gave a list of them as they existed at a much later date, and
drew therefrom the conclusion that there was no lady-chapel. I now
add the lists I have since found. The first is drawn from an inquisi-
tion taken of all the chantries of Southwell before the Prior of
Thurgarton and one of the Canons, in 1372; by authority of Abp.
Thoresby. The second is taken from the deed of surrender of the
college to Henry VIII. in 1540. The third from the *Certificate* of 37
Henry VIII.

I.	II.	III.
S. Thomas the Martyr	Thomæ Becket	Thomas Beckette
S. Peter	S. Peter	S. Peter
S. Nicholas	S. Nicholas	S. Nicholas
S. Stephen	S. Stephen	S. Thomas the Apostle
S. John Baptist	S. John Baptist	S. John Baptist
S. John the Evangelist	S. John the Evangelist	S. John the Evange-
S. Mary [the Virgin]	S. Michael	Our Lady [list
	S. Mary Magdalene	Marie Magdalene
	S. Cuthbert	Our Lady & S. Cuth-bert

The deed of surrender omits all mention of the chantry of Our Lady,
though it appears in each of the other two lists, and inserts in its
place the chantry of S. Michael. This may have been done inten-
tionally, for there can be no doubt about the existence of the lady-
chapel. Between the year 1372 and the reign of Henry VIII. two
new altars had been erected, those dedicated to S. Cuthbert and S.
Mary Magdalene. In other respects the lists agree, except that the
chantry of S. Stephen is omitted in the Certificate, and that of S.
Thomas the Apostle inserted.

of them groups of figures are rudely sculptured in bas-relief, raised from a quarter to half an inch. The sculpture has suffered somewhat in the removal of the plaster from the capitals. The one exception, the middle capital on the south side, shews the lamb and the dove among floral ornaments. On the capital west of this the subject represented is clearly the Triumphal Entry. The subject of the third capital is not so manifest. According to Mr. Planché* it "appears to repre-"sent either the nativity or the resurrection, according to the "opinion that may be formed of the central object, resembling "equally a cradle and a sarcophagus, surrounded by persons "who are raising their hands in adoration." But I am inclined to think that here we have a double subject repre-sented, and call attention to the figure of an angel, which Mr. Planché seems to have overlooked.

The capitals on the north side have representations of the Last Supper and the Twelve Apostles. The sculpture on the middle capital on this side is more interesting than any of the others, although it has not yet been satisfactorily explained. The interest centres in the figure of an ecclesiastic attired *in pontificalibus*, an archbishop or bishop probably, who is seen within a building saying Mass. He is standing beside an altar which has a chalice, covered with a corporal, upon it, but with neither lights nor cross. This was the common representation of the 12th century. Mr. Planché suggests that the sculpture may be meant to represent Abp. Thomas II. consecrating the church of which he was the founder, but, as this archbishop held the episcopate only from 1109—1114, it is unlikely that the church was consecrated until some years after his death. A group of four figures occupies the central part of the capital. Judging from the discs, it appears that three of these represent the Trinity, while the fourth is the figure of a man (who may be meant for Paulinus, the original founder of the church, as Mr. Planché again suggests) bending reverentially before them. The Father is represented with wings, one wing upwards, the other downwards; the Son, as an Infant, resting in the left arm of the Virgin, whose right hand holds what seems to be a staff. Beyond this group again are two other figures, one of a female, holding a lily, which may be a repetition of the Virgin, to whom the church is dedicated, the other of a child.

---

* See Paper in Journal of *Brit. Arch. Ass.* for January, 1853.

I have met with no notice of a sculptured representation of the ecclesiastical vestments of earlier date than the one before us, which cannot be later than the early part of the 12th century. Indeed I believe Mr. Ewan Christian has expressed an opinion that the capitals may have belonged to the former church. The ecclesiastic, whoever it may be meant to represent, is vested in the alb, stole, amice, and chasuble, with the maniple hanging from the left arm. The chasuble is a peculiar one—very short in front and coming to a point, but long behind. It bears a close resemblance to the chasuble worn by Archbishop Stigand, as represented in the Bayeux Tapestry. The archbishop wears the pall also, and in the figure before us there are certain lines on the front of the chasuble which may or may not be intended for a pall. There are some lines above the head which I at first thought to indicate a tall pointed mitre, but I am informed by Mr. Bloxam that the early mitres were bonnet-like, and do not always appear on the heads of bishops in the 12th century. With regard to the chasuble, the few effigies we have of the latter part of the 12th century shew them to have been worn very long at that period, while the earlier form was much shorter, at any rate in front. So it appears in the representation of a bishop in the Anglo-Saxon *Pontifical* in the library at Rouen.[*] Built up in an external wall of Bathampton Church is an effigy in bas-relief which Mr. Bloxham considers to be the sepulchral effigy of John of Tours, the first Bishop of Bath (died 1123). Here the chasuble is very short in front, coming to a peak.[†] The sculptures on these capitals are so full of interest that I hope before long they will be fully examined by some one more competent to explain them than I am.

THE SS COLLAR.—In the wall of the south choir-aisle there is an inserted Perpendicular doorway, now blocked up. From the character of its mouldings and ornaments its date has been assigned to the early part of the 15th century. The hood-mould terminates in two heads: one is a recent restoration, and the other, which is original, is crowned and affords an instance of the SS collar, the badge of the Lancastrian Princes. It was assumed by Henry IV., probably many years

---

[*] Described in the 25th Vol. of the *Archæologia*.

[†] Mr. Bloxam's *Companion to Gothic Arch.*

I

before his accession, and by him was certainly distinguished
as a Lancastrian ensign.* It occurs as early as 1382 in a
monumental brass in Little Chesterton Church, Rutlandshire.
It was common throughout the first half of the 15th century,
and occurs also as late as 1526 in a monumental effigy in
Elford Church, Staffordshire. There is a characteristic example, dating c. 1440, in Hoveringham Church, Notts. With
regard to its origin, it is generally supposed to have been
intended to represent King Henry's favourite motto, Sovereign,
by repeating the initial letter of the word. In the canopy
above the monarch's monument in Canterbury Cathedral, the
shield of Henry IV. is encircled with a collar of SS, after the
manner of the Garter of the Order. It appears also in the
effigy of Queen Joanna. The usual form of the collar shews
a series of the letter S in gold, the letters being either linked
together, or set in close order upon a blue or white ribbon,
which is suffered to lie loosely upon the shoulders and
fastened in front, the ends being connected by two buckles
joined to a central link, generally trefoil-shaped, from which
depends a jewel, or, more rarely, a badge. The case before
us is interesting as presenting some marked variations of the
usual form. A considerable space separates the letters, and
the ribbon fits tightly round the throat fastened by a buckle,
and the end hangs down after the manner of the Garter.

Glazing.

The painted glass in the windows of the chapter-house has
for the most part been brought thither, either from other
windows in the Minster or from other churches. I am told
that early in the present century Calverton Church was
despoiled of some of its glazing, which was inserted in these
windows. They contain, however, "a few remnants of early
"Decorated glass of the reign of Edward the First. They
"consist chiefly of portions of tracery lights, and of the
"spires and crockets of canopies belonging to the lower lights.
"These crockets are identical in form to those carved in stone
"round the chapter-house. In one of the tracery lights of
"the second window from the east, on the south, is a small
"medallion of white glass; on which is represented a knight
"on horseback, tilting, with a long spear under his arm. He

* The information on this subject is drawn chiefly from Mr.
Boutell's work on *Heraldry*.

"is habited in a long surcoat which reaches below the knees,
"and is armed in a hauberk and chausses of mail. His helmet
"is surmounted with a crest, resembling the wing of a bird.
"In one of the opposite windows are remains of heraldic
"borders, consisting of the yellow castles of Castile, and of
"a white lion rampant on a red field."

This account by Mr. Winston* may be supplemented by
the investigations of Mr. Planché,† who tells us the white
lion rampant on a red field is the badge of John Wood Mow-
bray, Earl of Nottingham, and a later addition. The same
authority calls attention to what he considers to be a heraldic
subject in the north-east window. He describes it as "an
"oak tree (*vert?*) eradicated and sprouting (*or*), between six
"boars, three and three, accosted, passant (*argent*)," and
reminds us that "a stock of a tree couped and eradicated,
"*or*, with two sprigs issuant therefrom, *vert*," is said to have
been a badge of Edward II.‡ He goes on to say: "a boar,
"*argent*, is the well-known royal English cognizance, it being
"the favourite one of Richard III., 'that bloody and devour-
"'ing boar,' as Shakespere with his Lancastrian predilections
"has indelibly branded him. Sandford tells us this silver
"boar was a badge of the house of York, and that he had
"seen it subscribed 'Ex honore de Windsor'; but this does
"not satisfy us as to its origin. We have still to discover,
"supposing the statement to be fact, how it came to be chosen
"as the symbol, or badge, or device of the honour of Windsor.
"We have in this piece of glass six boars *argent*, three on
"each side of the eradicated oak; and, if the painting be as
"early as the reign of Edward II., or perpaps Edward I.,
"some clue to the derivation of the Yorkist badge may possi-
"bly be obtained from it." It is a note-worthy fact that the
same subject is similarly treated in the sculpture of one of the
capitals of the arcade in the south-east side of the chapter-
house. In this case there are only two boars instead of six.

A few heraldic borders of Perpendicular date may be seen
in these windows, taken, I believe, from the west window of
the nave. The "portion of a late Early English White Pat-
"tern," inserted in the east window, must also have come
from elsewhere.

---

* See Paper in the Lincoln Vol. of the *Arch. Inst.*, 1848.
† See Paper in *Journ. of the Brit. Arch. Ass.* for January, 1853.
‡ Harleian MSS., 1073.

The only other painted glass worth notice is that which fills the lower tier of windows in the east end of the choir. They are Cinque Cento* paintings of the French School, and represent the Baptism of Christ, the Raising of Lazarus, the Triumphant Entry into Jerusalem, and the Mocking of Christ by the Jews. To quote Mr. Winston again : " the first sub-"ject considered as a glass painting is rather poor, being weak "both in colour and shadow. The whole of this picture "below the knees of our Saviour is a modern addition, by the "late Mr. Millar, who adapted the glass to the present lights. "The three other subjects are effective and good ; particularly "the second, in which, by a skilful management of back-"ground, a striking effect of distance and aerial perspective "is produced. The third, as a composition of colour, is per-"haps the best. These windows, though less powerful, are "more brilliant than Flemish glass of the same period. As "Pictures they go far to establish the claim of Glass Painting "to be considered one of the Fine Arts." They were pre-sented to the church by the late Henry Gally Knight, M.P., and inserted in 1818. In a letter to the Ven. Archd. Wilkins, dated October, 1837, he writes : " I met with them in 1815, "in a pawnbroker's shop in Paris, where they had long "remained in a neglected heap in a corner. I was told, and " I believe it was true, that they came from the chapel of Le " Temple, where Louis XVI. was confined. Le Temple was "originally the mansion of the Knights Templar, and built "A.D. 1140." Between the years '20 and '25 the windows of the upper tier were filled with painted glass containing the armorial bearings of the King, the "late and present Abps. "of York," the Prebendaries, Gally Knight, and a few others. These were replaced in 1876 by windows presented by resi-dents of the town. At the east end of the north aisle is a memorial window to the last Prebendary, Mr. Thomas Henry Shepherd.

The Eagle Reading-desk.

The brass eagle which stands in the choir seems originally to have belonged to Newstead Abbey. About the middle of last century it was found in the bed of the lake in the Abbey grounds, and passed into the hands of a Nottingham dealer, from whom it was bought, in the year 1805, and presented to the

---

* The style prevailed the first half of the 16th century.

Collegiate Church by Sir Richard Kaye, Prebendary of Southwell and Dean of Lincoln. The Nottingham dealer found in
the hollow boss on which the eagle stands some documents
relating to Newstead Abbey. They had probably been placed
there and the eagle thrown into the lake for concealment in
the troubled times of Henry VIII. They afterwards passed
into the possession of the late Colonel Wildman. The story
related by Washington Irving, in his work on Abbotsford and
Newstead, that the contents of one of the deeds cast discredit
upon the monks of the abbey has been shewn to be mere fic-
tion. The following inscription is engraved upon the shaft:

𝔒rate pro ana 𝔎adulphi 𝔖abage et pro anabus 𝔒mn
𝔉idelium 𝔇efunctorum.

Pray for the soul of Ralph Savage, and for the souls of
all the Faithful Departed.

Lee's Pillar.

Reges et Reginæ erunt nutrices tuæ.
Hanc
Collegiatam et Parochialem Ecclesiam
Religiosa Antiquitas
Fundavit

Rex Henricus 8 Illustrissimus	{ restauravit 1543 }	Edwardo Lee Archiepiscopo Ebor. Piissimo	} Petente
Reg. Elizabetha Religiosissima	{ sancivit 1584 }	Edwino Sandys Archiepiscopo Ebor. Dignissimo	} Interce- dente
Monarcha Jacobus Præpotentissimus	{ stabilivit 1604 }	Henrico Howard Comite Northamptoniensi Prænobilissimo	} Mediante.

A Domino factum est istud:
Da gloriam Deo
Honorem Regi.
Sint sicut Oreb et Zeb, Zebe et Salmana,
Qui dicunt possideamus Sanctuarium Dei.
Psal. 83. 11.
Det Deus hoc sanctum sanctis; sit semper Asylum
Exulis, Idolatris Sacrilegosque ruat.
Gervas Lee
In piam gratamque Mæcenatum memoriam
Posuit.
1608.

This inscription until quite lately adorned one of the great piers which support the lantern tower. It tells us that Religious Antiquity founded this collegiate and parochial church, that Henry VIII. renewed the foundation, and that Elizabeth and James I. ratified and confirmed it; but it omits all mention of its suppression by Act of Parliament in the Reign of Edward VI. Indeed there are grave doubts as to the legality of its renewed existence subsequent to Edward's reign founded on the action of Queen Mary and her successors, for it seems never to have been supported by any Act repealing the Act of Suppression. There is an interesting letter in the Record Office written by James I. to Abp. Hutton, and dated August 16, 1603, in which the King states that, finding no royal residence near Sherwood Forest, where he will often have to pass in his journeys between England and Scotland, he wishes to make an exchange with the See of York for the houses and manors of Scroby and Southwell, which are conveniently situated for his forest sports. He urges the Abp. to consent, as the houses are much decayed and the tenure of Southwell manor is questionable, and promises to give full value for them and to establish the church at Southwell. The exchange was not effected. The King, however, did *establish* the church, in 1604, as Lee's inscription asserted.[*]

CHAPTER VI.

THE PALACE.—THE VICARS' COURT.—THE COLLEGIATE SCHOOL.

The Palace of the Archbishops of York has been little more than a ruin for more than two centuries. While the Scots lay before Newark, at the close of the civil war in the reign of Charles I., the Scotch Commissioners lodged therein, and when they withdrew their protection and marched northwards with the unhappy King, it was left to the tender mercies of the Parliamentary troops, who, stripping all the lead from its roofs and otherwise despoiling it, began the destruction which the elements were afterwards allowed to complete. Only one of the great apartments, the hall, standing in the north-west corner of the quadrangle, has been preserved; but enough of the exterior walls of the palace, with their windows and fire-

---

[*] See above, p. 33.

places, remains to reveal to us the general plan of what must have been a truly grand mansion. Two great gables, with large window-arches, flank the eastern wall. The northern one of these was probably the end gable of the chapel, which, with the hall, must have occupied a great part of the north side of the quadrangle. At the south-east corner remain the ruins of the tower or keep, and these contain a series of garderobes ingeniously arranged round a central pillar.* Attached to the south wall of the hall remains the jamb of a window-arch of unusually large dimensions. The hall is now being restored by the Bishop Suffragan of Nottingham. When the restoration was taken in hand it was found to have been divided into two parts by a partition wall, which concealed the eastern part of the fireplace; the eastern portion formed part of a dwelling-house, occupied, in the early part of the century, as Shilton tells us, "as a very respectable seminary "for young ladies," and the western portion at the same time served both as a Sunday-school room and as the court chamber where the Justices of the Soke of Southwell, nominated by the archbishop, held their sessions. Entrance to the latter was gained by stone steps leading to a doorway built into the lower lights of the west window.

Though no part of the existing ruins can be dated earlier than the latter part of the 14th century, yet there must have been a mansion here long before that time, for Southwell had been a favourite resort of the archbishops.† Dugdale, in the *Monasticon*, tells us that this palace was built by Archbishop Thoresby, *c.* 1360. In confirmation of this Mr. Parker has pointed out that the roll-moulding which runs round the walls and buttresses proves them to belong to the Decorated period. All the windows and fireplaces, however, are evident insertions of the 15th century. Indeed so many alterations and additions were made by Abp. Kemp (1425, 6—1452) and his

---

* A sketch, with plan, appears in Mr. Parker's *Domestic Architecture.*

† The residence of the Abps. of York, at Bishopthorpe, some 2½ miles from the city, was built by Walter de Gray in the 13th century. Aldred (died 1069) was buried at Southwell. Other archbishops buried here were: Godfrey de Ludeham (1264), Thomas de Corbridge (1304), William Booth (1465), Lawrence Booth (1480), Edwin Sandys (1588). Gerard (1109) and Godfrey are specially mentioned as having lived and died at Southwell. Geoffrey Pantagenet was ordained here in 1181, and Henry de Newark, before he became Abp. in 1296, was a Canon of Southwell.

successor, William Booth, as to give rise to the belief that the former was the original founder.* Cardinal Wolsey, also, spent much money in repairing and adorning the palace, though it is unlikely that any actual building of importance was undertaken by him.†

---

* "A copy of all such armes as be standing in stone, wodd, or "glasse, within the Biscoppes place at Southwell. First at the "entering of the Porche is graven the armes of Kempe, Archb. of "Yorke, who founded the said house."—Rawlinson MSS., Bodleian, Oxford. Dugdale, who visited the palace shortly before the civil war, gives an account of the armorial bearings it contained. They have quite recently been restored in the new glazing of the windows of the hall. Shilton in 1818 wrote: "at the east end [of the hall] "are the arms of the founder [Kemp], projected on the breast of an "angel; he bore three corn-sheaves, in allusion to his origin, which "was that of a husbandman's son, of Rye, in Sussex." This, which has suffered mutilation since Shilton's day, is likewise to be restored.

† References to Southwell in the State Papers under dates 1527—'30, afford instructive illustration of Wolsey's history. Thus in the days when his power was greatest we have a letter addressed to him by Lawrence Stubbs, President of Magdalene College, Oxford:— "The prior of S. Bartholomew's, Smithfield, is sick and likely to die. "The friends of William Finch, cellarer of the same, have offered to "give your lordship £300 for your college, at Oxford, for your favour "towards his preferment. Dr. Barrye, residentiary of Southwell, is "deceased, by whose death there is a prebend in York at your gift, "and other promotions" (1527). Under 1528 there is a letter by Wolsey "touching the condition of my manor at Southwell with the "parks and woods there." Then came his disgrace (August, 1529), accompanied by the seizure of his palace and plate at York Place, now Whitehall, and a command from the King that he should retire to his diocese. It seems that the palace at Southwell was not ready to receive him, but we find him dating letters thence in June of the following year (1530). A little later he left Southwell for Cawood, where he was staying at the time of his arrest under the *præmunire*. Under 1530 the following notices occur:—

1. William Claiburgh to Wolsey—from Windsor.—I have delivered your letters to Mr. Magnus, and told him what need you have of a house near Southwell for a season. your manor not being ready, suggesting that he should give up Sibthorpe.—And the letter goes on to speak of Wolsey's "poverty."

2. Robert Brown to Wolsey.—I have received your letter desiring that I should see your manor of Southwell repaired against your coming. I have got ready faggots for the kitchen, bake-house, and brew-house, and have ordered the mason to work the doors of your gallery, etc , and caused locks to be made for the servants' doors and houses. As for casting of your gallery with lime and hair according to the direction of Mr. Holgill your surveyor, there are no workmen that can work in that matter—and so on.

The Vicars' Court lies at the east end of the Minster yard. It forms a quadrangle, the west side being open, the east occupied by the Residence House, which used to be appropriated to the use of the canon residentiary for the time being, and the north and south sides each filled by two vicarage-houses. Two of the six vicars-choral lived elsewhere: the parish vicar in the parish vicarage, and the school master in the chantry-house, which I shall have occasion to speak about later on. The present buildings in the vicars' court were built in the year 1780, at which time the buildings they replaced, called *The Vicarage*, had long been in a state of decay and threatened immediate destruction to their inhabitants.

The College of Vicars, founded probably by Abp. Gray in the 13th century, had common domestic buildings before the year 1379. In that year Richard de Chesterfield, one of the canons, petitioned Abp. Alexander de Neville and obtained leave to appropriate a portion of the *cimitery* east of the church, and to build thereon a new mansion for the vicars at his own expense. Their dwelling-house, he said, threatened

---

3. Ric. Lyster (Chief Baron) to Wolsey.—I have received your letter dated Southwell, 19 June, and perceive you are discomfited at the process against you directed to the sheriff of Yorkshire.

4. Thomas Runcorn (priest) to Wolsey.—I told him [secretary Gardiner] the great necessity your grace was in, and begged him to solicit the King, out of respect to the service your grace had done him, that he would, out of consideration for your former and present estate, look upon you with charity, and relieve you from this miserable poverty—(1,000 marks for journey to North spent in paying debts in London, and Wolsey had to borrow)—that as for the magnificent buildings you were accused to making, they are nothing but the stopping of holes where it rained in from the windows, doors, etc., and had been paid by your receiver at Southwell out of his own money.

5. Cromwell to Wolsey.—For although your conviction in the *præmunire* is touched upon in the preamble, your pardon and restitution stand good, and you need be in no fear for your spiritual and temporal goods.—Then follows advice not to build at Southwell any more.

6. Inventory of Wolsey's plate and goods found at Cawood by the Earl of Northumberland.—£4,265 ought to divers persons at his departure from Cawood, and not yet paid.

The inherent love of luxury and display shines forth in Wolsey's character up to the bitter end. On the other hand there must have been something fundamentally good in the man to whom his servants remained so faithfully attached in the days of his disgrace and retirement.

ruin, so much so that they had to find separate lodgings in the
town, to the occasion of scandal abroad and the detriment of
divine worship in the church. Moreover it was some distance
from the church and the way was muddy and deep * So he
built a quadrangular college on the site of the Vicars' Court.
It seems to have been a stone building of one story, covered
with roofs of wood sufficiently high-pitched to form a second
story of apartments. Entrance to the quadrangle was gained
by an archway in the middle of the west side, and the east
side was occupied by the college hall.

In the year 1485 the roofs were replaced by a second story
by William Talbot, also a canon, whose sepulchral slab, lying
in the vestibule of the Minster, has already been described.
In the year 1689 the hall on the east side was taken down
and a Residence House built from materials taken from the
woods on the Norwood estate, granted to the chapter for the
purpose by Abp. Lamplugh. His successor, Abp. Sharp,
provided that the Vicarage should be divided into five houses
for the use of the vicars choral, the sixth vicar, being vicar of
Southwell, to use the parish vicarage-house. It seems that
the Vicarage, which had afforded shelter to the sixteen vicars
of olden times, was not large enough to give house-room to
the six vicars of later times, with their families, and some of
them had gone to live elsewhere in the town. Two rooms
were ordered by Abp. Sharp to be set apart for use as the
Registry.

Dickenson has given a description of the Vicarage as he
knew it before its destruction in the year 1780. "Natural
"decay in some instances, and the suggestions of modern
"convenience in many more, occasioned the most curious
"parts of this building to be taken down early in the last
"century but one—viz. the projecting windows, porches, and
"oratories, with which it abounded. Three only of these
"remained to our time. These were at the west end of the
"quadrangle—viz. one over the gateway into the church-
"yard; another contiguous to the north side of it, with a
"western aspect; and a third over the door of the north-west
"house looking into the quadrangle. The first and last of
"these had been oratories in the Roman Catholic times,
"Their ornaments ascertained their purpose as well as their

---

* Mr. Dickenson, without giving his authority, tells us it was
situated on the east side of Bullivant's Dyke.

"age: the end of every beam or trace terminating in the
"head or body of an angel; and every other place, which
"admitted of an ornamental piece of carving, being loaded
"with the two emblematic roses of the houses of York and
"Lancaster, in conjunction. The other projection was a bow
"window, much decorated with similar ornaments, and on
"the inside of the wall underneath it, in large characters,
"𝕎ilhelmus 𝕋albot."

The Collegiate School seems to have been founded early in
the 16th century, but the exact date of its foundation does
not appear.* It was endowed by Edward VI. in the amount
of £10 payable annually out of the exchequer. Before the
suppression of the college the mastership was always held by
one of the vicars choral, who received in addition £12 from
the chapter and £2 from the prebendary of Normanton.† All
boys born in Southwell were entitled to education in the
school free of expense; their number was usually about
twelve. Formerly two Scholarships and two Fellowships,
founded in the reign of Henry VIII., in S. John's College,
Cambridge, were appropriated to scholars of the Grammar
School who had served as choristers of the chapter of South-

---

* By the will of Robert Batemanson, proved before the chapter on
the 27th November, 1512, it appears that he bequeathed certain lands
at Egmanton to found a Free Grammar School at Southwell, the
master to receive 40s. yearly. If, however, the school should not be
founded within four years from his decease the property was to pass
to the Prior and Convent of Thurgarton. There is no record of the
fulfilment of the will, nor of the possession of property at Egmanton
either by the chapter of Southwell or the convent of Thurgarton.
It is to be noticed that the school is not mentioned in the foundation
deed of the fellowships in S. John's, Cambridge, quoted in the text
(in fra). They were founded in 1531. Very possibly the endowment
of Edward VI. marks the date of the foundation of the school.

† Queen Elizabeth, in her statutes, in order that piety and learning
might for ever in the church and neighbourhood more and more day
by day flourish and increase, ordained that one learned in Latin and
Greek, religious, honourable, studious, and skilled in teaching, subject to approval and confirmation by the Archbishop, or, the See
being vacant, by the Dean and Chapter of York, should be elected to
the Grammar School of Southwell, who should always labour to
instruct in letters as well as in manners, whose duty should be, not
only to read thoroughly, teach, and hear Latin and Greek Grammar,
but also to imbue the minds of the boys with the Ordinances of the
Christian Religion (quod fieri potest).

well. The terms of the original foundation runs thus :*
" Dr. Keyton pro duobus soc. et duobos discip. Paid for this
" foundation 400 *lib.* settled by Indenture Nov. ult. an. H. ෪.
" 24° Provided always that the said fellows and scholars be
" elect and chosen of those persons that be or have been
" choristers of the chappell [? chapter] of Southwell, if any
" such able persons in learning and manners can be found in
" Southwell aforesaid. And in default of such persons there,
" then of such persons as have been choristers of the said
" chappell of Southwell, which persons be then inhabitants
" abiding in the said University of Cambridge. And if none
" such be found able in the said University, then the said
" fellows and scholars to be elect of such persons as be most
" singular in manners and learning of what country soever
" they be, that be then abiding in the said University.—Dr.
" Keyton was Canon of Salisbury, and Archd. of Leycester."
Mr. Dickenson cites a case in 30 George II. in which one
Todington, chorister, appealed to the Bishop of Ely, as
visitor general of S. John's College, against the election, by
the master and senior fellows, of one Craven, who had not
been a chorister, to one of these fellowships. The master and
fellows moved in the Court of the King's Bench for a prohi-
bition, but the court ruled against them, and the Bishop
decided in favour of Todington, who was elected accordingly.†
This, with another similar case, was quoted by the University
Commissioners in 1852 in their Reports, in which they recommended that the appropriation of the Scholarships and Fellowships in question to choristers of Southwell should cease.
All such appropriations were abolished by the Statutes of
1860.

The Collegiate School, as it is now called, has seen many
changes and vicissitudes within the last hundred years.
Previous to the year 1784 Booth's Chapel, which stood on the
south side of the Minster, occupying the second bay of the
nave, was used as a school-room. In that year the chapel

---

* Quoted from *Reports from Select Committee on Education,* 1818.

† The kindness of the Senior Dean, the Rev. A. F. Torry, has
supplied me with a list of the holders of these Fellowships. It is too
long for insertion here, but I may notice a few of the names that
occur in it: William Becher (1764), Sherard Becher (1808), Chappell
Fowler (1726), Charles Fowler (1781), Benjamin Clay (1784), Prof.
Blunt, William Pound, and W. C. Evans. Holders still living are
Messrs. W. S. Wood, A. M. Hoare, and Burbury.

was ordered to be taken down, and a room in the Red Prebend,* or Oxton *altera pars*, which occupied the site of the
Assembly Room, was hired as a temporary school-room. A
few years before this, when The Vicarage was rebuilt, the
vicar-choral who held the mastership was "fixed in The
Chauntry," and in 1791 a school-room was built in the south-
west corner of the churchyard. The Chantry was partly, if
not entirely, taken down about 1820,† and the present school
buildings erected upon its site in the north-west corner of the
churchyard. The government of the school is now in the
hands of the commissioners. I know nothing of its present
condition, but presume that it is better than it was in the
year 1837, when the chapter decreed that the choristers should
be instructed at the Endowed School at East-thorpe, and gave
"£30 to Mr. Massey in consideration of the present state of
"the Collegiate School."

CHAPTER VII.

SOUTHWELL: PAST AND PRESENT.

Little is known of the early history of the town of Southwell. Roman remains seem to have been found here in
sufficient quantities to justify the view that it is the site
of a Roman town.‡ It is all that can be said of it. Mr.
Dickenson, indeed, in his *History and Antiquities of Southwell*, wasted much argument to prove that it should be
identified with the *Ad Pontem* mentioned in one of the

* According to Shilton, in the year 1818 as many as ten of the old
prebendal houses remained in Southwell in various degrees of preservation. For particulars I must refer to his *History of Southwell*.

† Before the Reformation the chantry priests formed an independent corporate body, and apparently lived together. I have before
me a plan of the buildings as they existed in the year 1818. The
chantry was a red brick building, enclosing a court some 70 ft. by 50
ft. The plan shews also several buildings at the extreme west end of
the churchyard which were pulled down in 1822. These include a
parish vicarage-house, the school-room. and the "Castle Inn."

‡ See Appendix B.

Itinaries of Antoninus Augustus as a Roman station on the great road leading north through Leicester and Lincoln—the Foss Way. It seems that no such station ever existed.* If we can accept as a historical fact the tradition that S. Paulinus established here, early in the 8th century, a missionary centre for the conversion of the Mercian settlers, it seems only likely that he chose the spot on account of its then being an important settlement, and where, maybe, he found the remains of a former British church.

Its very name, variously spelt Suthwell, Sudwell, Suell, seems to imply an existence previous to the inroads of the Danes from East Anglia into this part of the country, which took place towards the end of the 9th century. The old street-names of Southwell are sufficient evidence of the exten-

---

* I am indebted to the Rev. R. F. Smith for the solution of this question. The *Itinaries* are quoted from Mr. Petrie's work:—

I. *Iter* a Londinio Lindo .. M.P. CLVI. *sic*,
Verolami [*S. Albans*] ........M.P. xxi.
* * * * * *
Ratis [*Leicester*] ....
Verometo [*Willoughby*] .... xiii.
Margiduno [*East Bridgeford*] ...... xiii.
Ad Pontem [?] .... vii.
N.B.—Another MS. has xiiii
Crococalano [*Brough, nr. Collingham*] vii.
Lindo [*Lincoln*].................. xii.

II. *Iter* ab Eburaco Londinium M.P. ccxxvii.
* * *
Lindo...........................
Crococalano .... xiiii.
Margiduno .... xiiii.
Vernemeto xii
* * * * * * *

The *iter* going south is without doubt the correct one: it omits *Ad Pontem*.
Against the correctness of the *iter* going north:—
(1) Two successive marches of only 7 miles each very improbable. I find no parallel instance in the *Itinaries*.
(2) Discrepancy in the MSS. Another MS. gives distance of Crococalanum from next station south of it as 14 instead of 7 miles, thus agreeing with the *iter* going south.
Explanation: *Ad Pontem* probably only a marginal note affixed to Margidunum, denoting this is the spot where one has to branch

sive settlement of the Danes in and about Southwell;* and from that time, at any rate, it must have assumed the proportions of an important town. But there is no documentary evidence of its existence of earlier date than the reign of Edwy in the middle of the following century, when that monarch made the Archbishop of York and his successors lords of the manor of Suthwell. Nor have we any absolute testimony to the existence of a church here before the middle of the 11th century. But the grant of Edwy implies as much. Leland, indeed, tells us that "ther was a Se at Southwell of "the Merches which now longeth to tharchbishop of York."† But it certainly was not a separate See at the time of Edwy's grant of the crown lands to the Archbishop of York, and had it ever been so some more certain evidence of the fact would be forthcoming.

---

off *to gain the bridge* across the Trent. Mistaking this marginal note for a distinct station some ignorant scribe would easily insert it as such, and, to tide over the difficulty of the omission of distance, would divide the distance of Crococalanum from Margidunum, 14 miles, into equal distances of 7 miles each.

East Bridgeford lies between the road and the river, close to both, and over against it is Gunthorpe Ferry. Bridgeford denotes *the ford where there was once a bridge*—a Roman bridge, doubtless, which in Saxon times fell into bad repair and ultimate disuse, the Saxons being no bridge-builders. Margi-dunum signifies *gypsum-hill*, and the presence of gypsum in the vicinity of East Bridgeford confirms its identity. Crococalanum has been identified by topographical writers with Brough, which formerly occupied a spot on the right hand of the road some 3½ miles from Newark.

* Farthingate, Back Lane, Petticoat Lane, Bar Lane, and Moor Lane may still be identified. These, with Church Street, Burgage, Westgate, and the adjoining hamlets of East-thorpe, West-thorpe, and Normanton, make up the present town. Pottergate, Milnegate, and Prestgate, are the names of streets which have either disappeared or their situation is not now known. Pottergate is mentioned in a deed dated 21 Edward I. (Thoroton's *Nottinghamshire*). Milnegate is mentioned in the *Registrum Album* under date 1393; Prestgate, Westgate, and Farthingate, under 1496. Under various dates in the reign of Edward II. there is mention also of an open piece of ground called the Dyrsing or Dersing Meadow (Shilton's *History*). Thoroton tells us "the scite of the town of Southwell is divided into two parts, "the Burgage and the Prebendage: the former comprises all that "part of the town between the market-place and the river Greet; "and the latter the Prebendage and Church."

† "Southwell town is metely well builded, but there is no market "public. The minster of our lady is large but of no pleasant build-"ing, but rather strong."—*Collectanea.* (Leland died 1552.)

In Southwell and its neighbourhood, in early times, there
were four parks the property of the Abps. of York. The
Southwell or Little Park, about 130 acres, lies south of the
town, running close to the palace. Hexgreave Park, comprising some 700 acres and lying about four miles north-east
of the town, is now divided up into farms. *Bokesgrave* Park,
Thoroton tells us, was acquired to the See by Abp. Walter de
Grav in the reign of Henry III. The same abp. built the
original palace at Bishopthorpe, near York. The third park,
called Hockerwood or *Hokerwood* Park, about a mile north-
east and containing 120 acres, was granted "among other
hereditaments" to the Earl of Warwick by Edward VI. after
the suppression of colleges and chantries. Norwood Park,
comprising some 100 acres, close to the town on the west side,
is still intact. About the middle of last century it passed
into the possession of Mr. John Sutton, by whom the present
red brick mansion was built, and the estate became freehold
in 1778, when Sir Richard Sutton procured an Act of Parliament enabling him to exchange for it certain lands with the
See of York. All the property of the abps. were alienated
from the See during the civil wars of Charles I's. reign. The
principal purchaser was one Edward Cludd, who bought
the Palace, Little Park, and Hexgreave Park for the sum of
£1,666 7s. 3½d. Norwood Park passed into his hands, and
Thoroton, writing a few years after the Restoration, tells us
that he "built a pretty brick house upon it, and since his
"Majisty's return, is become tenant to the Archbishop, as I
"guess," for at the Restoration all episcopal estates reverted
to the Sees to which they had belonged. Mr. Edward Cludd
raised himself to a position of influence in the county during
the civil war, in which he took a prominent part on the side
of the Parliament. The idle boast of his confidential servant
at this time was that "he and his master ruled all Nottinghamshire." Under the Protectorate he became Justice of the
Peace and Knight of the Shire; and the story of "Cludd's
Oak," in Norwood Park, tells of his custom of celebrating
the rite of marriage under its branches, after the manner of
his time.*

---

* A small slab in the Minster has "E. C. 1672" upon it. This has
been wrongly pointed out as marking the burial-place of Edward
Cludd, for it appears from the Rolls Court Book that he served on a
jury at Southwell as late as the year 1676.

The meaning of the name of Southwell is self-evident.
Norwell is some eight miles distant.* There are four historic
wells of Southwell. First the Lord's Well, in Southwell
Park, famous for its healing properties. The Holy Well,
situated in the open court adjoining the cloister in the Minster.
Lady's Well, in the Minster Yard, some few yards east of the
chapter-house. This well was covered over in 1764 in consequence of a Mr. Fowler meeting his death by falling into it
on a dark night. The fourth well was called S. Catharine's
Well, near a chapel dedicated to that saint, which formerly
stood in West-thorpe. There were several other chapels in the
town or neighbourhood, and the remains of one of these, I am
told, still stand in Normanton.

Tanner, in his *Notitia Monastica*, tells us that there was a
hospital dedicated to S. Mary Magdalene in the year 1313.
In early times there were many hospitals in the country,† and
they served much the same purposes as our almshouses in the
present day serve. They were nearly all suppressed in the
reign of Edward VI. I have found only two other notices of
this hospital at Southwell. The State Papers, under 1532,
contain memoranda of the archbishop's possessions at Southwell, and among them appears the following: "The patronage
"of Southwell College and all the prebends and chantries.
"The patronage of the hospital of S. Mary Magdalen in
"Southewell." An inventory of church goods, *temp.* Edward
VI. contains the following item: "as for the magdalene
"chapell yt ys sold by the Kynge and pullyd down to the
"grownde."

The history of the Saracen's Head Inn, which faces Church
Street, is full of interest. Thoroton cites a deed, dated 19
R. II. (1396), wherein the house is described as the messuage
lying between the mansion of the Prebend of Oxton and
Crophille, and the messuage sometime Henry Atte Barres.
The Assembly Room now stands on the site of the prebendal
mansion referred to. *Barre* is the old word for a gate,
Henry atte barre was a convenient way of distinguishing
the Henry who lived in the gate-house. The exact position
of the gate-house cannot now be recovered, but *Bar Lane*

* At the time of the Domesday Survey the canons had property at
Norwell, and there was a church there.

† For list see Dugdale's *Monasticon* (1817-30).

x

was, until lately, the name of the modern Queen Street.* To return to the Saracen's Head, it seems to be a 14th century house. It is rectangular in shape, and built round a court which measures about forty yards by ten. It is entered through an archway in the east front, which contains a pair of massive oak doors. The building has a king-post roof of open timber work. In each truss the tie-beam is slightly curved and rests on side-posts with braces. The side-posts are also slightly curved inwards at the top. A pair of canted braces rises up from the tie-beam to the king-post, which supports a collar beam. One of the oak staircases still exists in a very tumble-down state. The wooden partitions which divide the habitable part of the upper story into rooms seem to be original and enriched with carving, but they are at present hidden by plaster and paper. The front of the house, too, is covered with plaster and shews none of its ancient features.

Charles I. lodged in this Inn on several occasions before and during the civil war.† Cromwell, too, is said to have occupied the very same apartments as those in which his unhappy victim lodged. This was on the occasion of his passing through Southwell on his journey north to suppress the renewed rising of the defeated Royalists in conjunction with the Scots.‡ . We are told, also, that the Inn was the

---

* We cannot too strongly deprecate the prevailing system of replacing the old names of streets by high-sounding modern ones. Many an ancient land-mark has been thus defaced and lost to memory. Town Councillors, too, should be careful to preserve the ancient spelling of these names. Thus *Micklegate*, in the City of Lincoln, has lately been dedicated to the memory of S. Michael by being repainted *Michaelgate!*

† These visits caused a change later on in the sign of the Inn from the Saracen's Head to the King's Arms for a time. Dr. Stukely, in a letter dated from Stamford, May 3, 1746, wrote of the Saracen's Head Inn: "The Inn is still remaining, though the sign is changed." And the same letter tells us how "the King's Arms were done upon "the gable end" of a house in Stamford in which the King had lodged soon after the battle of Naseby. A square stone, set diamond-wise, and bearing the King's Arms and the date 1693, may now be seen on the front of the house. This was found in 1797 on the removal of an old sign of the Saracen's Head which had been for many years placed against the wall.—Shilton's *History of Southwell*.

‡ His soldiers used the nave of the Minster as a stable for their horses. It is said that Cromwell issued a warrant for the destruction

scene of the "sorrowful parting" of the Queen and the
Royalist leader Cavendish, shortly before the defeat and death
of the latter in an engagement with Cromwell's Ironsides
before Gainsborough.

The following verses from the pen of Bishop Selwyn, who
wrote them after spending a night in the Inn, are worth
quoting on account of the local allusions. They are entitled
A Sleepless Night at Southwell.

> I cannot rest—for on the spot
>   Where I have made my bed,
> O'er-wearied with the strife of state,
>   A King hath laid his head.
>
> Thy sacred head, ill-fated Charles,
>   Hath lain where now I lie ;
> And thou hast passed in Southwell Inn
>   As sleepless night as I.
>
> I cannot rest—for o'er my mind
>   Come thronging full and fast,
> The stories of the olden time,
>   The visions of the past.
>
> 'Twas here he rested ere he raised
>   His standard for the fight ;
> Here called on Heaven to help his cause,
>   My God! defend the right !
>
> Here gather'd round him all the flow'r
>   Of England's chivalry ;
> And here the vanquished Monarch closed
>   His days of liberty.
>
> I cannot rest—for Cromwell's horse
>   Are neighing in mine ear ;
> E'en in the holy house of God
>   Their ringing hoofs I hear.
>
> Lord ! wilt Thou once again endure
>   In stable vile to be,
> The proud usurper's charger rein'd
>   Fast by Thy sanctuary ?
>
> I cannot rest, for Wolsey's pride,
>   And Wolsey's deep disgrace—
> The pomp, the littleness of man—
>   Speak from this ancient place.
>
> Here gloriously his summer days
>   He spent in kingly state ;
> Here his last summer sadly pined,
>   Bow'd by the stroke of fate.

of the nave and all such portions as were not necessary for the purposes of the parish, and that it was only the influence of Mr. Cludd
that saved the venerable fabric.

How mighty was he when he rul'd
  From Tweed to Humber's flood !
How lowly when he came to die,
  Forsaken by his God !

I cannot rest—for holier thoughts
  The lingering night beguile,
Of the glad days when Gospel light
  Went forth o'er Britain's isle.

'Twas here the Bishop of the North,
  Paulinus, pitch'd his tent,
Here preached the living word of God,
  Baptising in the Trent.

Hence have the preachers' feet gone forth,
  Through all the county wide ;
And daughter-churches have sprung up,
  Nursed at their mother's side.

Here have the clerks of Nottingham,
  And yeomen bold and true,
Held yearly feasts at Whitsuntide,
  And paid their homage due.

Here many a mitred head of York,
  And priests and men of peace,
Have lived in penitence and prayer,
  And welcomed their release.

And hence the daily choral song,
  The Gospel's hopes and fears,
Have sounded forth to Christian hearts,
  Beyond a thousand years.

'Tis thus, o'er England's hill and dale,
  Hath passed by Heaven's decree,
A changing light, a chequer'd shade,
  A mingled company.

The good, the bad, have had their day,
  The Lord hath worked His will ;
And England keeps her ancient faith,
  Purer and brighter still.

Where are they now, the famous men,
  Who lived in olden time ?
They never see the noonday sun,
  Nor hear the midnight chime ;

They sleep within their narrow cell,
  Waiting the trumpet's voice :
Lord ! grant that I may rest in peace,
  And when I wake—rejoice.

W. SELWYN.

Saracen's Head Inn,
   5th March, 1842.

Nottinghamshire played an important part in the civil war.* Western and Northern England sided with the King, the Midlands and the Eastern counties with the Parliament, and the central position of the county gave it great stragetic importance. The rivalry, therefore, between the lower and the upper classes was very keen. It was on Standard Hill, in Nottingham, that Charles unfurled the royal standard, but the county town very soon after shewed a preference for the cause of the Parliament and became one of its strongholds. Newark, on the other hand, remained loyal throughout, and, though closely besieged by the Parliamentary troops, and later on by the Scotch army, and more than once reduced to great straits, it held out to the end. When the battle of Naseby, June, 1645, seemed to have decided the issue of the war, in the following October Charles retired with his guards to South-well in the hope of once more rallying his supporters around him. Tradition tells us the story of how he one day walked into the shop of a boot-maker in the town, James Lee by name, who refused to serve his royal customer, pleading in excuse that he recognized in him the man of whom he had been forewarned in a dream that the hand of fate was upon him, and that no one would prosper who did anything for him.

Hearing that the garrison of Nottingham had become aware of his presence in Southwell and was determined to effect his capture, Charles quitted the town in haste only two hours before the arrival of a troop of horse from Nottingham. In the following March, when the King was shut up in Oxford, Cardinal Mazarin, "the cool Italian who ruled France," sent an emissary to treat with the Scots on behalf of the King. Montreville arrived in Southwell on the 26th of that month and took up his residence at the "King's Arms," as the Saracen's Head was then called, the Scotch Commissioners occupying the archbishop's palace. In consequence of the negotiations that passed between them the King determined to join them, and he effected his escape from Oxford in the disguise of a servant, with one or two followers, on the 4th of May. Two days later he arrived at Montreville's lodgings, sent for the commissioners, and after dining with them at the Saracen's Head, formally gave himself up to them, and was

* *Coritani Lachrymantes* is the title of a short history of the civil war in Notts., written about 1671 by a Mr. Savage of Southwell.

led to the Scotch army lying at Kelham before Newark. To the great disgust of its loyal inhabitants, the gallant garrison of Newark surrendered itself at the command of the King, and the Scots a few days later began their march northwards with their royal prisoner. Southwell, soon after, was occupied by the Parliamentary troops under Edward Cludd.

Notwithstanding the occasional visits of the King, the inhabitants of Southwell seem to have favoured the cause of the Parliament, and the Church and its prebendaries must have fared badly in the unfortunate period of the Protectorate. General Monk, on his way from Scotland to London to restore the monarchy in January, 1660, passed through the town, and there is a story—characterized by Shilton, the local historian, as "a barefaced falsehood, and in the very teeth of "history"—that he was greeted from the churchyard wall "with great store of blessings, prayers, etc. for the success of "his enterprise." In the State Papers, under 1660, we find a number of petitions to the King for preferment to vacant prebends. The notice of one of them is couched in the following terms:—Petition of Dr. Daniel Vivian to the King for the Prebend of Southwell belonging to Norwell Palishall, dio. York—he having been an army chaplain under the late King, ran great risks in the conveyance of letters, and has been a severe sufferer in the cause.

This was not the first civil war in which Southwell played a part. Five hundred years before, in the troubled period of Stephen's reign, it helped William Peverel to wrest Nottingham Castle from the hands of the Empress Matilda's followers. This William Peverel was the son of the mysterious Sir William Peverel of much disputed parentage, the "Peveril of "the Peak" and founder of the famous Honor of Peverel, who was appointed constable of the Castle of Nottingham by William the Conqueror. The younger William Peverel was a sturdy supporter of Stephen, and while he was absent with the King at the siege of Lincoln one Ralph Paganal or Pagnall, one of the Empress Matilda's captains, admitted the forces of the Duke of Gloucester into the town and castle. The Duke, much in want of money to pay the soldiers, determined to sack the treasury of S. Mary's, Southwell, and sent over a small detachment for that purpose. But the walls of the Minster-yard were well manned with gallant defenders, who successfully drove back their assailants to go and seek further aid from Nottingham. But, without waiting for their return, two young men from Southwell Mills co-operated with William Peverel, scaled the castle rock, and drove the Empress' followers out of Nottingham.* William Peverel then seized upon the castle and town, which were royal property, and on his refusal to surrender them, Henry II., who had meantime become King, expelled and disinherited him.†

Whatever be the opinion formed of the part Southwell played in these civil wars, there can be no doubt that its inhabitants in later times have been remarkable for their loyalty. In the troublous times that followed the French Revolution, in response to the appeal of the Government to the Lord Lieutenants that they should raise corps of yeomanry for the defence of the country in view of the threatened French invasion, the sum of £118 was subscribed for that purpose in Southwell. This was in 1794. In 1798 again a further subscription of no less than £275 was raised. The great volunteer movement of 1803 also extended to Southwell, and the Loyal Southwell Volunteer Infantry, under the command of Major William Wylde, had a muster roll of 243 members. The corps was disbanded in 1808.

The Burgage Manor House,‡ from 1804 to 1807, was the residence of Lord Byron's mother. Straitened circumstances had compelled the poet to offer for sale Newstead Abbey, "the last vestige of his inheritance," of which he was so proud and which had been in the possession of his family since the dissolution of the monasteries. The Pigots lived in a house on the opposite side of Burgage Green. Byron, at that time at Eton, spent his holidays here, and on his leaving school passed a whole year in Southwell. It was now that his strangely complex nature began to shew itself, with its intolerance of domestic restraint, its capacity for strong attachments, and its love of boyish freaks. It is said that Mr. John Thomas Becher, Prebendary of South Muskham, took much notice of him, and exercised sufficient influence over him to induce him to suppress the first copies of his

---

* See *Local Notes and Queries*, No. 163, in *Nottingham Guardian*.

† Mr. W. H. Stevenson in *Old Nottinghamshire*.

‡ The Burgage is a distinct manor, and in Shilton's day the Abp. as lord of the manor held court-leet in the Manor House twice annually, viz. on Thursday in Whitsun-week and on S. Thomas' Day, his steward presiding.

youthful poems, *Hours of Idleness*, published in 1807, on account of the too warm colouring of one of them.

The tone of society in Southwell in the old coaching days, like that of most of our small towns, was highly convivial. The Assembly Room,* the centre of the social gatherings, was almost nightly the scene of dances, dinner-parties, and the like. It was also used as a news-room, and once a week mine host of the Saracen's Head provided two packs of cards for the amusement of the more sober-minded. Southwell possessed a Theatre also,† in which Byron himself played, it is said, with great applause. These amateur theatricals were held in "old prebends and dilapidated barns, which for some "years were the only accommodation Thalia's sons could "obtain for the display of their histrionic talents," until, in 1816, a Theatre was fitted up.

These institutions have given place to those more adapted to the spirit of the times. The Literary Institute stands in the Market-place; it has a library of nearly 5,000 volumes, and a reading-room, where lectures are delivered in the winter season. For the benefit of the poorer classes there is a Free Library and Museum in Queen Street. This was founded by Mr. Jonas Bettison Warwick, formerly a medical man in practice at Southwell, who bequeathed £1,500 to trustees for the purpose, as well as his collection of minerals and fossils and a library of books.

This brief sketch of the history of Southwell may be closed with a notice of Holy Trinity Church, in Westgate. Under 1843 the Chapter Records contain a note :—It is expedient that a District Church be erected in Westthorpe : that the patronage be vested in the Bishop of Lincoln. It was consecrated in 1846. The cost of building and the endowment were quickly raised by subscription, the lists being headed by Mrs. Heathcote and Mr. H. C. Stenton. The parsonage-house was built in 1847.

---

* Built in 1805 by Mr. Richard Ingleman, who built also the House of Correction fronting Burgage Green. A curious account of the original Bridewell, built in 1606, and its management, may be found in the *Gentleman's Magazine*, Vol. 76. A short time back the prisoners were removed to Her Majesty's Prison at Nottingham.

† I have before me one of the original play-bills, dated July 20, 1804.

APPENDIX A.

COLLEGIATA ET PAROCHIALIS ECCLESIA.

It occurs to me that I have failed to lay sufficient emphasis on the double character of the church at Southwell as being both collegiate and parochial (see pp. 6 and 37 *foot-note*). This double character is preserved even in the present day. And here I have to correct an expression I used in an early part of this book when I described the church as being now, and until the erection of the bishopric, "merely parochial." So long as the last vicar choral of the college remains at his post, performing duties wholly distinct from those of the incumbent of the parish, the church will retain a remnant of its collegiate character. We have no clue as to which was the earlier institution, the parochial or the collegiate church. Mr. James Parker has called my attention to a passage bearing upon this subject in the bull granted to the canons by Pope Alexander III. in 1171. *Cæterum, si quis parochianorum vestrorum, vel etiam parochianorum Eborum Ecclesiæ infra cimiterium Ecclesiæ vestra*, etc. "But if any one of your parish-"ioners, or any one likewise of the parishioners of the Church "of York within the churchyard of your Church," etc. This passage by itself would lead one to conclude that there was at that time a parochial church *(ecclesia Eborum)* standing in the churchyard of the collegiate church, and distinct from it. This, however, we are fairly certain was not the case in 1171, though two churches may have stood side by side before the 12th century church was erected.* It must be remembered that *ecclesia* had a double meaning, being sometimes used to denote the actual building, at other times to denote the Christian assembly or congregation. It must also be remembered that in conventual churches the nave was often devoted to parochial uses. The passage quoted is an interesting record of the double character of the church at Southwell in early times, if nothing more.

---

* *See* App. B, p. 156.

APPENDIX B.

ROMAN REMAINS AT SOUTHWELL—THE TESSELATED PAVEMENT RECENTLY DISCOVERED IN THE MINSTER.

I have said (see p. 141) that Roman remains seem to have been found at Southwell in sufficient quantities to justify an argument for Roman occupation. The most important of these discoveries were made some few years after Dickenson published the first edition of his *History*, and in his second edition he gave an account of them. In breaking up a piece of ground, he writes, under the eastern side of the archbishop's palace, in the year 1793, to make a garden for one of the gentlemen of this church, a tesselated Roman floor was discovered of considerable extent, accompanied by several fragments of urns. These were found at the depth of five or six feet from the surface. In laying down a part of the flat pavement on the north side of the church, a little anterior to the time last mentioned, the workmen accidentally broke into a small vault, which, on the most scrupulous examination, was found to have been constructed almost entirely with Roman bricks. In the year 1794 one of the oldest prebendal houses in the town, situated on the north side of the church, was pulled down: in the walls, especially near the foundations, were many Roman bricks mixed with other materials; and scarce any of the more ancient buildings of the place have shared a similar fate, but in the foundations, at least, many Roman remains have been discovered. Mr. Dickenson also tells us that several Roman coins were in his day dug up on the south and east sides of the town. Among them were coins of Maxentius and Constantine; and he adds that many others, especially of the later Emperors, had been discovered in the vicinity of Southwell.

Since the second chapter of this work was written and printed the floor of the transepts has been taken up for repairs, and Mr. Petit's remarks, quoted on p. 52, have proved to be misleading. His story of a discovery of "a few years ago" must have been a tradition of many years. The spot indicated by him as the site of some ancient foundations of rubble work is occupied by the vault of the Fowler family, which dates back into the last century, and has swept away whatever old work there may have been there before it. In fact the transepts are so full of vaults as to have lost all traces of early work except along the west wall in the south transept. Here the workmen have discovered the remains of a mosaic pavement, its level being some ten inches below the general level of the floor of the transept. Its preservation seems due to the presence of a double row of 15th century seats which stand along the wall supported upon low cross-walls of brick which themselves rest upon the pavement in question. It was found that the paving of the transept did not run underneath these seats, the space underneath them being full of mould and rubbish. The *tesseræ* vary in size from ¾ to 1½ inches. Some of them are made from Roman brick or tiles, others are of stone in different colours, those of a light red and a very dark colour being most numerous. The remains measure 15½ ft. in length, their breadth varying from 1½ to 2 feet. They are not sufficiently extensive to shew anything like a complete pattern, but a close examination reveals two or more segments of circles, slightly larger than a semicircle, some nine or ten inches in diameter, the chords of which rest upon a narrow border-line consisting of a double row of the cubes made from red tiles. These segments consist of a series of concentric circles, in which the different stones are used without any regard to their colour, enclosing, in one case, a central square of the dark-coloured stones, five on each side, the central stone itself being a red one and somewhat larger than the others. Circles of larger diameter touch those just described, small portions only of which remain. Beyond the narrow border-line, which runs parallel with the west wall of the transept, no pattern is visible, and the remains vanish at about 2½ feet from the face of the wall. They give one the idea of having formed part of the border of a large pattern, but there is nothing to prove it did not extend beyond the transept wall. About four feet from the south wall there is a fragment of what appears to be the return border-line. This consists likewise of a double row of red tiles, but on each side of it there runs an additional row of very small white stones.

The pavement fails at present to throw much light upon the history of the church. Judging from the material, shape, and disposition of the *tesseræ*, it may have belonged to any building up to the 12th century. To my mind the level alone is sufficient argument against its being a part of the original floor of the present structure (12th century). Tesselated pavements were generally used by the Romans for the floors of their buildings. And since there is reason to believe Southwell to have been the site of a Roman town, it is quite possible that the pavement may have belonged to a Roman villa, the site of which was afterwards accidentally chosen for that of a church; or it may have belonged to a Roman Basilica.

On the other hand, it may have belonged to a Saxon Basilica. For there is no reason why, when the building art revived in the 7th century, the pavements should not have followed the Roman rule as much as the churches. And they doubtless followed the same rule in England till the 11th century, and in a few instances even later still as they did on the continent. Examples in churches occur, shewing more or less complete patterns, at Westminster and Canterbury, also at Fountains and Rievaulx Abbeys, and elsewhere. Fragments of Roman brick are worked up into the foundations of the eastern parts of the 12th century church in sufficient quantities to make it almost certain that the 11th century church only replaced one of earlier date on or near the same site. The same argument favours the view that a church existed here earlier than the 10th century also. Without presuming to *fix* a date for the pavement, all things considered it seems likely that it belonged to the Saxon Basilica which preceded the 11th century church, whether that Basilica be assigned to the 10th or the 7th century. The view that it is not actually Roman is in some degree confirmed by the fact that some of the *tesseræ* which are made from Roman tiles are not cut so squarely as others. The question, however, could only be settled by excavations on a large scale on the north side of the church, which I believe would be productive of considerable results.

Mr. Parker, with a view to including the pavement in the original church, kindly sent me a rough plan illustrating what he thought might have been the gradual extension of Southwell Minster. In the rough plan, a Saxon church, built *more Romano* in the form of a Basilica, occupies the site of the south transept of the present church and extends eastward of it. This would be either an early Saxon church, which would be parochial only, or a church of the 10th century, which might be either parochial only, or both parochial and collegiate. The 11th century church, collegiate, 1050—1060, also a Basilica, stands on the north side of the former one, and extends eastward from the piers separating the fifth and sixth bays of the 12th century church (*see* Plan II.) Before the 12th century the rule was to build beside of rather than instead of a church which was to be superseded. This appears, as far as evidence goes, to have been the plan adopted at Winchester for instance. Then comes the 12th century church (as in Plan II.), which would absorb both the Saxon churches; and lastly the 13th century extension.

APPENDIX C.

CHRONOLOGICAL TABLES.

Edward the Confessor....	1042	Edward II.	1307
William I................	1066	Edward III.	1327
William II.	1087	Richard II.	1377
Henry I.	1100	Henry IV...............	1399
Stephen	1135	Henry V.	1413
Henry II.	1154	Henry VI.	1422
Richard I...............	1189	Edward IV.	1461
John	1199	Edward V...............	1483
Henry III.	1216	Richard III.	1483
Edward I...............	1272	Henry VII.	1485

Henry VIII............. 1509—1547.

	1050		
Early Norman	—	1066	Norman.
	1125	—	
Later Norman	—	1145	Transition.
	1175	—	
Transition ..	1189	1189	Lancet.
Early English	—	1245	
	1272	—	Geometrical.
Decorated....	—	1315	Curvilinear.
	—	1360	
	1377	—	Rectilinear.
Perpendicular.	1547	1547	

The above divisions of styles are those adopted by Mr. John Henry Parker and Mr. Edmund Sharpe respectively. Roughly speaking the Norman, Early English, and Decorated styles may be said to belong to the 12th, 13th, and 14th centuries respectively, the transition to each style occupying in each case the previous half century.

INDEX.

160